THE KIDNAPPED PRODIGY

RICHARD NORMAN

A DAN GOOD MYSTERY

CHAPTER 1

September 1, 1986

It was dusk. Nineteen year old Mandy Lynn entered Rock Creek Park at the water-powered Pierce Mill entrance and drove to her regular parking spot. Rock Creek Park bisects the Northwest quadrant of D.C. It is a large and beautiful park, heavily wooded, and with many trails, it is a popular place for joggers. She left her car and headed out.

To keep her long dark tresses from whipping around, she'd pulled her hair back into a ponytail. Dressed in jogging shorts, sports-halter and running shoes, she set off.

Armed with mace and a whistle, she felt secure. There had been two joggers along the trails that had gone missing in the past three months. She'd read about them just this morning in the Washington Post.

As she'd run about a mile and a half, she glanced at her watch, and saw she was not quite making her desired speed. She started picking up her pace, but in that distracted moment, when she had glanced at her watch, she was suddenly struck hard on her head and fell to the earth, stunned. Still semiconscious, she heard only faint unintelligible sounds, and felt the sting of a needle in her shoulder. Then, big rough hands picked her up and carried her. She tried to rouse and felt for her mace, but it was gone and so was her whistle. The sound of a car trunk opening filled her with sudden fear, but before she could think, she was dropped onto what could only be the floor of a car's trunk. The lid closed, and she slipped into unconsciousness.

CHAPTER 2

Monday, September 2, 1986

The next morning, when she woke up, Mandy felt as though no time had passed at all. Her eyes opened, and she looked around, expecting to be where she had fallen. Where was she? She was in a very nice bedroom, but it wasn't hers.

Now she began to remember. She'd been hit in the head. She felt around, and found a big knot on the back of her head. It was still very sore. Then she remembered being carried, and tossed in the trunk of a car. Who had done this? Why? What day is it? What time is it? Where am I? She looked at her wristwatch, but it was gone. Glancing around the room, she saw there were no clocks anywhere.

This bed. It was very comfortable. She was covered with a sheet and warm coverlet. She noticed a closet across the room. The door was ajar, and she could see clothes hanging inside; feminine clothes. Suddenly she lifted the covers to see how she was dressed. A pretty nightgown, but way too short. Who changed her

clothes? Not some strange man, she hoped.

Am I ok? Physically?

She felt no pain, so she thew back the covers and stood by the bed. Her legs were not wobbly; she wasn't shaking. She didn't think she'd been raped, so she sat on the edge of the bed. It was a fine looking four-poster. The furniture looked high grade; the room was nicely furnished. She saw a large sit-down dresser with a big round mirror. She got up and went to sit before the mirror. Her hair was clean and only a little tousled from sleeping on it. Her skin felt clean. She smelled her arm. It smelled of lilacs. Someone had bathed her and washed her hair. She felt very uncomfortable, but she got up to go checkout the closet. Only dresses were there, no slacks or jeans. There were also nightgowns and shoes. Five pair of shoes on the floor beside her running shoes; three pair of sandals, and two high heels with three-inch heels. She counted six dresses and six nightgowns, including the one she was wearing All the dresses were nice and exactly her size. However, only three of the nightgowns were long. She didn't like them so short, but she could wear panties when she wore the short ones, she guessed. She looked through the dresses, and selected a nice print and matching sandals. The room had its own bathroom, so she went in to take a shower. After dressing and doing her hair, she went to the chest of drawers. There, she saw her jogging outfit clean and folded. There was a stack of bras and panties all in her size, and three slips. No stockings. None of the clothes were hers. She pondered her situation.

Why was I kidnapped? Ransome? I don't think they would keep me in such a nice place, provide such nice clothing for me and take good care of me if they were going to kill me. What on earth is going on?

She sat down in a nice armchair. Then she realized she was hungry. She looked around and saw the room had no windows, so she would never know if it was day or night. She wondered again where she was, what time it was, and what day.

The door! She jumped up and rushed to the door. It was locked just as she feared. She wasn't surprised, she was a prisoner, but why? She went back to sit in the armchair. The same questions went around and around in her head.

Why, me? And who? Who would want to kidnap me? How long have I been here?

It startled her to hear a key turn in the lock. Then it opened and a big, burly, ugly-looking creature of a man came in cautiously. When he saw Mandy in the armchair, he turned and motioned to someone behind him. A tall, slender woman entered carrying a tray. The food was covered with a large white linen napkin. The woman looked to be about forty or so, and was attractive. She wore a stylish dark blue dress and black pumps with a two inch heel. She wore no jewelry, not even earrings, and no rings on her fingers.

"Breakfast," was all she said, and that in English, but she had some kind of an accent; maybe German, she thought. The woman laid the tray on a small table with a straight-back chair; a place to sit and eat. Then the woman turned to follow the large apelike creature out.

"Wait," said Mandy, but they ignored her and left. The door locked behind them. Mandy sat at the small table, and removed the napkin to find a nice omelet, two slices of buttered toast, two slices of bacon, salt and pepper, a small container of strawberry jam, coffee, a small pitcher of cream and two packets of sugar.

It must be morning.

Everything was still hot, and the food was delicious. She was ravenous.

Wow!

As she ate, she thought the brute was just muscle to subdue her had she tried to escape or fight them.

I bet he was the one that kidnapped me.

The woman had a nice face, but she seemed foreign, somehow. What was it? She didn't know. Had she been taken by foreigners? Was the creature also foreign? Was she already in some other country? That thought terrified her. If she was not overseas, would she be taken overseas? In two weeks she was scheduled to perform four of Beethoven's piano sonatas at Carnegie Hall in New York.

Surely, mom and dad know I've been kidnapped by now. I think it is the FBI that works kidnappings, so I hope they are looking for me, and will find me soon.

A single tear ran down her right cheek. She sniffed and straightened up her back, and frowned.

I'm not going to cry, I'm a big girl. It's strange I haven't been hurt or mistreated. They've treated me kinda like royalty so far. I don't understand what is going on?

The key rattled in the lock again. This time three people entered; the same creature, the woman, and a big man very overweight. He wore a black business suit, white shirt, black necktie, and black patent shoes. He looked older than the woman, perhaps ten years or more, and he was very tall; way over six feet.

This time she noticed the muscle man. His face looked like it

had been badly beaten at some time in the distant past. He wore brown slacks, and a T-shirt that showed off his muscular arms and chest. His hair was black and wild, as though he'd
just come out of a wind tunnel. He wore
heavy brown work boots.

The woman took her tray and left. Now she gave her attention to the big fat man. His face was flabby, but, at the same time, seemed pleasant. His graying hair was receding; nicely trimmed and short.

Mandy waited for him to speak. The muscle-man stood on the alert with his massive arms crossed.

"Good morning miss Lynn. I regret I cannot introduce myself or any of us just yet, I'm sure you understand why."

He spoke with a German accent, she was sure. Perhaps they are all three Germans.

"Where am I? Who are you people, and what do you want with me?" She yelled at him, and muscle-man took a step toward her, but the fat man held up a hand to stop him.

"I will tell you nothing," he said calmly. "Come with me."

"No," said Mandy. "I'm not going anywhere with you."

The fat man's face clouded with anger. "You will!" he shouted. "You have no choice in the matter. It is time. Now!"

Mandy ran to the four-poster bed and wrapped her arms tightly around a post.

"I'm not going anywhere with you. You can't make me."

Muscle-man came and pried her arms off the bedpost as she kicked him and screamed bloody-murder. His strong arms picked her up and tucked her under one arm to carry her kicking and screaming out of the room.

She struggled hard, but it was nothing for him to carry her down a short hall to stairs, and down. In her efforts to escape his clutches, Mandy did not notice the house; the well-appointed hallway, nor the beautiful stairway. He carried her into a large empty room where he set her down on a cushioned bench. Only then did she notice the grand piano. She was sitting on a piano bench. There were three other armchairs near the piano. This piano must be close to nine feet long, she thought. A Kawi. One of the finest of pianos, but it wasn't new. It looked used. Then she suddenly noticed sheet music stacked on the side of the piano. She was dumbfounded.

The fat man said, "It is time for you to practice."

CHAPTER 3

Monday, September 8, 1986

GOODWOODS was the name Ben Good had given to his estate on Georgetown Pike in McLean, Virginia, a suburb of Washington, D.C. He purchased the place in 1921 when he was invited to Washington to serve in Warren G. Harding's administration as Undersecretary of State. He was a millionaire oil man from Dallas, and he was a brilliant undersecretary. Ben and his wife, Bea, were killed in an auto accident in 1955. Their only son, Dan, inherited his father's great wealth and this estate.

At times, Dan and his wife of just over a year, Kathleen, lived in the big mansion on Turtle Creek

Boulevard in Highland Park, a suburb surrounded by Dallas. Dan owned "Good Investigators," the largest private investigation company in the southwest. He was a young retired CIA agent.

He and Kathleen alternated staying in the mansion in Dallas, and staying in the mansion in McLain, Virginia.

Dan and Kathleen were married last June, and in July of this year, she announced that she was expecting. Dan was 42; Kathleen, 24. They had come to the McLean estate for a six week's stay. There was a permanent staff in McLean, and in Dallas. Mr. and Mrs. Wilson stayed with the home in Dallas, but they'd brought their newly hired nanny, Barbara Shaw, with them to McLean so Kathleen could continue tutoring Barbara to get her GED.

The staff at GOODWOODS was larger than in Dallas. There was much more property to maintain. There were the stables with five horses, and the grounds covered five acres. The area along Georgetown Pike was heavily wooded. GOODWOODS backed up to a corner of the estate of Bobby Kennedy.

The house was well back from the road. Massive trees filled the yard out front, and a row of trees along the roadway helped form a long section of a beautiful leafy canopy over Georgetown Pike, a beautiful drive. It was less than a mile from Goodwoods to CIA headquarters. Occasionally, Dan was hired as a freelancer by the CIA. In fact it was on just such a case that Dan met Kathleen, and they fell in love.

It was after the wedding of Paige, Dan's secretary, on September first that they came to McLean. Paige had married Jon Cameron, and resigned as Dan's secretary to be a fulltime homemaker. Dan would find a new secretary after their stay in Virginia. His business in Dallas was run by his old friend, Robert White, President of the corporation. Dan only came to the office as he wanted. He was retired, but still kept his hand in things at the office. Dan was now chairman of the board.

Here, in McLean, Dan did not want or need a butler. Phil Wilson had been the butler in the Dallas address since before Dan was born.

It was 9:17 a.m. when the door chimes sounded throughout the enormous house.

"I got it!" yelled Dan since he was near the front door.

His next door neighbor, Tom Lynn was standing there. He looked a bit disheveled, and his eyes were red like he'd been crying. He was a small man, about five-six, thin, with a receding hairline. His blue shirt was wrinkled, and his sleeves were rolled up to his elbows. He wore jeans and scuffed dress shoes.

When he saw Dan, he looked down and ran a hand through his hair. "Hello, Dan. I heard you came up. Welcome back. May I talk to you?"

"Of course, Tom, anytime. Come in. Want some coffee?"

"No thanks, I'm practically floating in it."

"Let's talk in here," said Dan as he led im into a nearby sitting room. He closed the door for privacy, and they sat. "I can see you're troubled. What's the matter?"

"Dan, my daughter's been kidnapped." His voice broke, and he began crying,

Dan was shocked, "Mandy?"

He nodded.

"Tom, I'm so sorry. When did this happen?"

He struggled to get himself back under control. Finally, he took a deep breath and said, "It happened on the first of this month. She runs most every evening at Rock Creek Park... I... I don't know where to turn or what to do. The FBI is looking for her, and, of course the police, but they tell me there are no clues... they have no leads. She's just vanished."

"What can I do to help, Tom?"

"Would you? Could you? I know your reputation with the CIA,

and I know of the success of your company in Dallas. I believe you may be our best chance. Better than the cops or the FBI. Mary and I talked about this just yesterday. It was her suggestion that I come over to ask you. You know we can pay."

"Tom, you and Mary have been our neighbors and friends here for a very long time. I remember when you got Mandy. I don't need to be paid. You are a good friend, and Mandy is important to me, too. Such a sweet young lady, and so talented. A child prodigy pianist. I remember when she made her debut at the Kennedy Center at age 13. She played Beethoven's fourth piano concerto as I recall. Brilliant. I'll find her for you, I promise."

Tom sighed deeply. "Thank you, Dan. I feel better already." He stood. "The FBI doesn't seem to be making any progress. Mary is a wreck. She couldn't come with me."

Dan stood. "I understand. Give her my regards." Dan put an arm around his shoulders as he walked him to the door.

"I want to take a look at the crime scene in a little while, and I'll need you to show me where it is. I'll call you when I'm ready to pick you up. Try not to worry too much."

He left.

When Dan turned from the door, Kathleen and Barbara were standing behind him.

"Tom looked awful," said Kathleen.

"Mandy's been kidnapped. He and Mary want me to find her."

"That is terrible," said Kathleen, "but that's a big part of your business; finding missing persons."

"Yes," said Dan. "I want Brenda to come up for a few days to help."

"And *me*," said Kathleen. "I can help."

"Not this time sweetheart. You're carrying our precious baby now, and you still need to help Barbara with her studies. By the way, how are you doing, Barbara?"

"I'm doing great. I love it. Kathleen is a wonderful teacher. She makes everything so clear and easy for me. You two have really changed my life, and I thank you, again. Actually, I am overwhelmed by your generosity. I never dreamed my life could be this good."

"Oh, poo, Barbara. You are *very* smart. You just never had a chance before. I have no doubt you will pass your GED, and get a college diploma, too, if you want. Come on, let's go back upstairs to work on your grammar studies before lunch time."

Barbara was still suffering from her broken collarbone and broken ribs. Her face was still bruised and scared from the beating she had received from a john when she was a prostitute. Dan and Kathleen had rescued her from that life. Now she had a new chance at life as Kathleen's nanny. It was nice to see her so upbeat.

As the two ladies went back upstairs, Dan could hear Barbara say, "I've never been out of Texas.

Virginia is so beautiful. And this place... " He smiled. It seemed she was making good adjustments to her new life

Along this stretch of Georgetown Pike were many large estates. There were several with equestrian equipment between the road and the houses, and often one could be seen on horseback practicing jumps. Dan owned horses as did Tom. They rode, but neither had need for equestrian equipment.

He went to his study and called Brenda. Then he called Tom to tell him he would pick him up in a few minutes.

When Dan drove up to the house, both Tom and Mary were out front waiting. Mary was near the front door, and when she saw Dan drive up, she hurried back inside. Tom opened the passenger door and slid in.

"You know Rock Creek Park," he said, "I'll direct you to the scene when we get there." Tom looked much more presentable than before.

"I take it Mandy no longer lives at home if she jogs in Rock Creek Park."

""Yeah, she moved to an apartment just off Grover right after her nineteenth birthday. We've been very concerned about her safety, but what could we do? We bought her a smaller grand piano for her apartment. Still it was a struggle to get it up to the second floor; a five foot grand instead of her nine foot grand at the house."

"I bet," said Dan.

"I really miss her practicing her pieces and arpeggio's night and day. Don't know if you know, but her abduction is the third in that area over the past three months."

"I didn't know."

With difficulty, he added, "We don't know if she is dead or alive." Tears rolled down his face again.

"Have you had no ransom demands?"

"No. Not yet. Two FBI agents are at our house in case someone *does* call. That is what concerns me most; no ransom calls."

It heightened Dan's concern as well. No ransom indicates no intention to return her.

Dan wondered, why was she taken? She was a beautiful young lady, but was it for human trafficking, or something else? She's a famous concert pianist. Did that have anything to do with it?

They entered Rock Creek Park, and Tom said, "The FBI has been all over this, of course, but I doubt they know anything. They've never told us much of anything."

Moments later, he straightened up and pointed. "There, Dan, turn into this parking area. That is where her car was found."

"Let's take a look," said Dan. "I don't expect to find any clues the Feds missed; don't think they'd miss any. I just want to get a feel of the place. I suspect the FBI stomped all over the trail, destroying any clues I might find, but let's take a look anyway."

"I remember Mandy telling us she ran three miles, and I told the FBI." About a half down the trail, the ground showed a lot of scuffing activity in the dirt. They said they believed she was taken at that point," said Tom. It did indeed show some activity, and Dan spent some time looking around.

"They brought me here, Dan. Her abductors parked in the lot, so there are no tire tracts."

Dan replied, "I think her abductors must have been watching her for some time to see what her habits were, then they must have made plans to wait for her. They likely surprised her, subdued her in some way, and carried her to their car. Very simple."

"They? You think there was more than one?"

"Yes, Tom, I think there were at least two to be able to carry it off so well."

"They found her car, and can of mace barely off the trail. Somebody had stepped on it to crush it. Her whistle was found in some bushes over twenty yards away. I guess one of her abductors threw it there."

"I suppose they've talked to all her friends and acquaintances," said Dan.

"Yes, as well as our friends and neighbors and even her piano teacher and members of the Symphony Orchestra members."

"Hmm," said Dan.

He wandered around another fifteen minutes. He went pretty far into the surrounding woods and thrashed about some. Then he came back and started walking along the trail away from the scene very slowly.

Where is he going? wondered Tom.

Dan went almost out of sight. Then he bent over to look at the ground. When he straightened up, he turned, and walked briskly back.

"Ok, Tom let's go home."

On the drive home, Dan said, "I found something that may be significant. I don't know if it has anything to do with Mandy's kidnapping or not, it was so far away from where she was taken."

"What did you find?"

"I walked almost a hundred yards, looking very carefully, but saw nothing. Then as I turned to come back, I noticed something small and white just off the pathway. Cigarette stubs. There were only two, and they had been stepped on and ground into the dirt, so someone didn't just throw them casually away along the trail, they had stopped. Neither were very white, and they were barely showing through the dirt, but I spotted them and picked them up just in case.

"Often, the kinds of people that do any kind of criminal activity are smokers, and many of them know they should not leave a cigarette butt at a crime scene. Many have been caught because cigarette butts are sometimes good clues, but I walked a very long way away from the scene. Farther, I think than most investigators would normally think of going. I do that because I believe smarter criminals might do that.

"These butts may be someone else's, but it's worth a look. If these are the kidnapper's, then they may be foreigners."

"Foreigners?"

"Yes. Possibly Germans, but I'm not certain. The cigarette butts had part of the brand name on the paper. I recognized the brand. It was barely discernible, but I know that brand is made in Germany; it is also popular in other European countries, so I can't be certain."

"Wow," said Tom.

"This is a very long shot, Tom, so I'm not sharing this with the FBI. They would not want me involved anyway, and would try to stop me."

CHAPTER 4

Tuesday, September 9, 1986

The Washington Post was laid next to
Dan's place at the breakfast table
each morning when he came to
Goodwoods.

As was the custom there, the
staff at Goodwoods gathered for
breakfast every morning at 6 a.m.
Kathleen insisted she cook most
meals when she was there. She loved
to cook and was proficient.

Dave and Alice Stevens
managed the estate in McLean, and
Alice cooked when Dan and Kathleen
were in Dallas. Dave and Alice were
in their late forties, and had been
caretakers for the past eight years.
They lived in the mansion, as did

Baxter Stone, the groundskeeper; single and twenty-seven.

Butch Hargraves, an ex-jockey, took care of the horses. He and his wife, Flo, and their two small children, Tim and Terry, lived in the bunkhouse, which was not a real bunkhouse, but a small cottage on the estate near the stables. Now that Dan and Kathleen and Barbara Shaw, Kathleen's nanny for her expected baby, had come, it was a happy and vociferous bunch that came to the breakfast table; chattering and laughing.

After a big breakfast, the staff dispersed to their daily duties, and Dan and Kathleen were alone. Dan picked up the newspaper, and one of the main stories on the front page bore the headline, "**Missing Rock Creek Joggers Found Dead.**"

"Listen to this, sweetheart," said Dan,

"Marie Greggory and Connie Valentine, two of the three missing Rock Creek Park joggers, were found in a dumpster behind a fast food restaurant late last evening. They had been beaten and strangled. It has not been disclosed yet whether they were molested. Miss Greggory was an instructor in a local gym. She was single and living with a boyfriend. He was unnamed, but is a person of interest in both murders. Miss Gregory is survived by her aunt and uncle who raised her, and a younger brother. She was twenty-five years old. Connie Valentine, a thirty-one year old bar tender, was also single, and lived alone. It is not known if she had any family survivors. The third missing Rock Creek Park jogger, Mandy Lynn, remains missing.

There is more to this article, but there is another article just about Mandy. It has a large photo of her. I hope she is still alive, and we can find her before she gets killed."

"Oh, Dan. I wish I could help."

"I'll be sure to keep you as my Chief Advisor, sweetheart. You are always a great help to me, honey. I wish I could help find the killer of the other joggers. I hope Mandy doesn't end up dead in a dumpster."

"Speaking of Mandy, what time will Brenda arrive?"

Dan looked at his watch. "Ten-twenty. Dulles is not too far from here."

"It'll be nice to see Brenda again."

"Since we have some time, what would you like to do, sweetie?"

Kathleen looked at him, cocked her head and said, "Well....... "

CHAPTER 5

Kathleen insisted on tagging along to the airport. They were at the gate in plenty of time.

When Brenda came out Dan thought he should be careful to call her by her new name, Brenda White. She and Robert White, president of Dan's company, were married back in August. She'd said August was the perfect month, because, if her husband wanted to snuggle in the hottest month in Texas, he really loved her.

Brenda was 58, and Bob was 61. Both had snow white hair. Brenda's hair was beautifully quaffed, and naturally curly. It fell just above her shoulders. She had lost some weight, and now had a very nice figure to go with her lovely face. Brenda was head of the research department in Dan's company: Good Investigators. They picked up her baggage, and went to the car. Brenda kept her attaché with her, and laid it beside her on the back seat.

"I've set up my den at the house for us to use as our base of operation," said Dan. "I am anxious for us to get started."

"I think you were right, Dan," said Brenda, "about Mandy's kidnappers being German. I've been doing some digging, and it seems American cigarettes dominate many European countries, so a German brand is a bit unusual in America, to say the least. I have other things that I want to share, but I'll wait till later."

"That *is* good news, Brenda. After lunch, we'll all get situated in our workspaces."

***

I've been forced to practice about eight hours every day on that old piano. I don't know exactly how long they make me practice; I can only guess, because they took my watch, and I've seen no clocks anywhere.

Fat man and the woman seem to be a couple, though he looks older than she, and they sit and watch and listen to me practice. The creature sits some distance away and glowers. I think he may be deaf, he never speaks, but the couple speak German to each other though they both speak English, too. I don't know any names, yet. I might recognize a German name if I heard one, but I'm not sure. The pieces they insist I work on are the ones I'm to play at Carnegie Hall. Why? They have taken very good care of me, fed me well, and I sleep well. No one has ever hurt me.

I think they may be going somewhere. It appears they may be packing. I am afraid they may take me with them if they don't kill me first. I'm scared to death they will take me to Germany. I could be in Germany

now, I don't know. I am always afraid they will kill me, or hurt me, and the thought of leaving the US terrifies me. I don't want to go anywhere overseas. I've never wanted to even perform anywhere overseas. At least not yet. Maybe later when I'm older. Of course, I have been invited to perform overseas, but have always declined. I wish I could get to a phone and call my parents, but if there are any telephones in this big old house, I haven't seen one. I'm restricted as to where I can go. Only to my room, and the piano room. I wish I could contact someone someway. She thought for a minute.
    Hmm, maybe I can.

CHAPTER 6

Lunch was at strait up noon, and after lunch, Dan, Brenda, and Kathleen retired to Dan's den.

"Alright," said Dan, "let's hear what you have, Brenda."

Brenda was wearing a long sleeved navy dress with white polka dots and sensible shoes with a two-inch heel. She opened a manilla folder, and took out some papers.

"As I told you in the car, I believe it might well be that Mandy was taken by Germans. I do think it was more than one person. Of course we can't be certain it wasn't someone from some other European country because that same cigarette brand is also sold in France, Denmark, and Sweden. Possibly other countries, too, but I rather think the kidnappers are from Germany."

"Why," asked Kathleen.

"Simply because the cigarettes are made in Germany. I had my team do some intensive probing into locating Germans that have moved into the D.C. area in the past three months."

"Why three months," asked Dan?"

"Just a hunch that it is someone new to the DC area, and we found three."

"Three? That's too easy," said Dan. "Surely there are more than just *three*."

"I had them go back just to July 1," Brenda replied. "There were more, but as I checked each party, I narrowed it down to three. They are not far from each other, either. There are a bunch of rowhouses near the German Embassy over on Embassy Row."

"Ok, if you say so-," said Dan. For now he would just listen.

"Some rowhouses are purchased, and some are rented, or leased. We contacted the real estate agencies that rent and lease those rowhouses, but I selected only the places that have been *rented*. That is really why I have only three. One place was rented for a year, another for two years, but the third was a short-term rental of only three months. That is the one I think we need to check out first."

"I'm impressed. You do amazing work, Brenda," said Dan. "Remind me to give you another raise."

"That would be nice, but remember, this is all *assumptions*. We *assumed* those cigarette stubs were left by the kidnappers, and we are *assuming* whoever left them was from Germany. So we are *assuming* the kidnapper is German, and we are *assuming* that they rented the short-term rowhouse," warned Brenda. "We could easily be making false assumptions."

"At least it's a place to start," said Kathleen.

"Here are the addresses." Brenda handed Dan a piece of note paper.

CHAPTER 7

Mandy showered and dressed before breakfast was brought to her room. She was still locked in the bedroom. The fat man didn't come to get her for her daily practice this morning. Hours had passed, and she was still waiting,

Just then, a key turned in the lock, and the creature came in with the fat man right behind him. The creature stood by the door, and the fat man drew up the vanity seat to sit in front of her.

"I assume you have noticed we have been packing."

Mandy nodded once.

"You are going with us," he continued.

That set her off, "Where are you taking me, you big fat pig? And *why* did you kidnap me? Why do you make me practice my pieces I am to play at Carnegie Hall? What's going on? I want to go home!" She began to cry.

The fat man just looked at her sternly. "Get hold of yourself, young lady. Stop that crying! I forbid it! Stop right now!" He was shouting. She began to gain control, and soon she was just sniffling.

"I will tell you only what I want you to know," he said. With that, he stood and strode out of the room. The creature followed and locked the door behind them. Mandy sat in contemplation for a while.

If I'm leaving this place, I'd better leave something behind that will help people know I was here in this house. This is my chance.

She had a plan so she got up and went to the chest of drawers. The only thing that really belonged to her was her jogging outfit. Her halter top had a Neiman- Markus label, but it was very difficult for her to rip it out. Finally, with great effort, she managed. It helped that her fingers were trained to be little hammers on the piano; they were strong. Her mother would certainly know it was from her halter top; she had bought it for her. Again, she looked all around the room.

I expect they will scour this place before leaving it. Where can I leave it so I can be sure it is found?

She kept looking around the room thinking, and an idea formed in her head.

***

Dan said, "If you want, Brenda, why don't *you* take a car and check out the addresses. I think a woman would be less intimidating than a man or even you and me together."

"Fine," said Brenda. "What car should I take?"

"There are five out there, take any one you wish."

Brenda looked at Dan and grinned, "The Mustang?"

"Sure, why not.?"

She was thrilled. She grabbed her purse, and hurried out the door.

The foreign Embassies on Embassy Row in DC are mostly stately old buildings, well cared for and set in beautiful surroundings; big, tall trees, nice lawns and shrubbery. Most Embassy employees lived nearby in the surrounding area. Some streets off Embassy Row have rowhouses, and that was where Brenda found the address. She nudged the curb in front of a recently built set of rowhouses. Each house had a different facade and different colors, but this one was all white. Of course the one she parked in front of was the short-term rental.

Brenda's plan was just to inquire if a certain employee of the German Embassy lived there; a sniffing expedition. She chose the fictitious name, Hans Wagner. She planned to pronounce it as a

German would. She spoke no German.

She climbed out of the little Mustang, and casually walked up to the entrance. She carried her oversized purse by a strap over her shoulder. In it, her Glock was easily accessible. She punched the doorbell and waited.

When the door opened, a heavyset man in a pale-blue dress-suit and a blood-red necktie appeared. He was completely bald and wore wire frame grannie glasses. In very American English, he simply said, "Yes?"

Brenda was a little surprise, but responded like manner in English, "I beg your pardon, sir, but I am looking for a young man named Hans Wagner. He works at the German Embassy."

"There is no one here by that name; in fact there is no one living here at all now. They moved out this morning. I'm the rental agent."

"May I ask you a few questions, Mr..."

"Willingham, I'm Josh Willingham, and you?"

"Brenda White."

He noticed her rings on her left hand. "Come in, Mrs. White."

He led her to the livingroom which was fully furnished, and they sat in plush overstuffed chairs.

"Now what may I do for you? Are you interested in renting this place?"

She smiled her most winsome smile "I'm afraid not. Actually, I am a private investigator, and I believe the previous tenants kidnapped a young lady jogger from Rock Creek Park, and were holding her here."

He quickly responded. "Oh, I hardly think so. It was a wealthy middle aged German couple who had just arrived in our country with a manservant. They were looking for a place to buy, but not in this area. They called me last week to tell me they had changed their minds, and had decided to return to Germany. They'd paid their lease in advance.

They hardly looked like criminals."
He smiled.

"Most criminals don't look like criminals; you know it is said there is no *criminal* look."

"But middle aged wealthy people?" he objected.

"Perhaps," said Brenda, "but we think she was taken by Germans who have just recently come to America. May I ask their names? I would like to eliminate them as suspects to be sure."

"Well," said the real estate agent, "I suppose it's alright to tell you. Schmidt. Dietrich Schmidt, and his wife, Clara. The servant's name is Fritz Something."

"Hmmm," said Brenda, "Smith in English. A very common alias." She got a pen and note pad out of her purse and jotted down the names, anyway."

"I recall the story in the Post. Three joggers in recent months. Two were found dead, and the third was a famous young pianist."

"It is she we are trying to find."

"There is one thing that is strange."

"Yes?"

Mr. Willingham shifted forward in his chair and cleared his throat. "The Schmidt's *did* rent a very large grand piano while they were here. I assumed one of them played. They returned it this morning."

Brenda's heart nearly jumped out of her chest. She could barely contain her excitement, but she calmly asked, "Would you mind if I just looked around a bit while I'm here."

"Not at all," said Willingham. "I want that young lady found as quickly as possible. If it helps to find her, be my guest. Take all the time you need. I'll be here a while. This is a furnished house, and I'm here to inventory the furnishings to be certain they didn't take something they shouldn't."

"Thank you Mr. Willingham."

"No, no, just call me Josh, please."

She nodded, "Thank you, Josh. I should not be long. I think I will begin upstairs."

"Fine," said Josh.

Brenda picked up her purse, slung the strap over a shoulder and headed up the stairs. There were four bedrooms, each with their own private bath. There was also a larger separate bathroom. This was a large place.

Brenda entered the master bedroom first. She wondered if they left fingerprints. Dan would have to check that out, it wasn't in her expertise. She dug in her purse and found a pair of latex gloves and put them on. The room was good size, but not excessively large, and its private bath was commensurate in size with the bedroom. She moved around the room, carefully looking for... something. She didn't know what.

When she felt she was done, she went to the bedroom next to the master bedroom. It had not been occupied because all the furniture was covered in white cloth. Still, she searched this room carefully, but found nothing.

The third bedroom was furnished in a masculine fashion. She searched it just as thoroughly as the other rooms. If there were clues of any kind from anyone, she wanted to find them. Nothing.

Upon entering the fourth bedroom, it was obviously decorated with a woman's touch. Everything was feminine. There was a lovely fourposter bed made with a pretty duvet and fluffy pillows; a marvelous vanity with a big round mirror. She thought it odd that it had no window at all. Of course, there was nothing in any of the rooms except furniture.

If Mandy was kept in this room, there was nothing that said she was, but Brenda did a more intense search. She spent much time searching the closet and the room itself. Nothing.

She went into the attached bathroom. It was pristine. Nevertheless, she would assume nothing. As she looked around the toilet, she lifted the top of the tank to look inside. It was something that probably every detective would do. Normally they looked for evidence of drugs there, but Brenda's heart nearly stopped when she lifted the lid off the water tank, and a very small scrap of cloth drifted to the floor. It had been wedged between the lid and the edge of the tank. It had also been folded to make it more secure in its hiding place, but when it fell to the bathroom floor, it unfolded a little. She quickly picked it up for a close look. Upon opening the tag, there was something written on it; the logo of Neiman-Marcus.

CHAPTER 8

The rental car was a big Buick
station wagon. Fat man was driving,
his wife (Mandy assumed) sat beside
him. The creature sat with her in the
back seat. The rest of the space was
pretty well filled with baggage and
strong cardboard boxes that were
excessively sealed with waterproof
wrapping and bound with waterproof
tape. This puzzled Mandy.

They were on I-95 south. Fat
man and the woman were having an
intense conversation in German.
Mandy's hands were bound behind
her back, but her feet were free, and
she wasn't gaged. She decided she
would try again to find out where
they were going.

"Hey, fat man," she yelled. "Where are you taking me, you big, ugly slob?"

He said something in German, and the creature backhanded her in her mouth. It was hard enough to slightly split her lip, but not so hard as to damage her teeth.

Fat man said in English, "Shut up, or I will tell Fritz to hit you again much harder."

Ah. Fritz. I have one name at last.

After a while, they turned off the highway onto a narrow road Mandy didn't recognize, though she was trying to keep every detail in her memory to tell the police if she ever got that opportunity. She tasted only a little bit of blood, so her lip wasn't cut badly. It was the first abuse since the bump on her head.

The road was narrow and winding. Both sides of the road were treelined, forming a beautiful, leafy canopy overhead. She had no idea where they were nor where they were going.

The Fat man slowed, and turned into a long meandering driveway that wound deep into the woods. He stopped in front of another massive house. Its façade was white stone. In spite of its location in a wooded area, it looked very nicely kept.

"We are staying here overnight," fat man announced.

Mandy wanted to ask if they were going somewhere else tomorrow, but was afraid she would get hit again, so she said nothing.

They were greeted at the door by a small, rounded woman. She looked to be in her thirties, and over a modest gray dress, she wore a small, white apron with frilly ruffles. A personal maid thought Mandy. She led them into a strikingly opulent house. Furniture seemed handmade. Many antiques. Tall Ficus trees and large potted plants were everywhere. She ushered them into a posh parlor where stood a largish woman with steel gray hair cut like a man's. She was old, and wore a deep blue blouse; not tucked into black slacks. Her sneakers were large, black and clunky-looking. Some might refer to her as a handsome woman, but Mandy thought she was too mannish, and looked stern and unwelcoming. She certainly wasn't attractive. Mandy half expected lions and tigers to come out of so much shrubbery in the rooms. The walls had what appeared to be lovely original oil paintings; landscapes, each with gilded frames. They all sat in the parlor. Everyone spoke German, so Mandy understood nothing, but the sound of their hostess' voice was as unwelcoming as she looked. They seemed to be in a big disagreement over Mandy, because every few minutes, they would glance at her. After about ten minutes, fat man stood, leaned toward the older woman and spoke a few gruff words to her. She pursed her lips and gave a quick nod of acquiescence. Fat man spoke a few words to the creature who went out to the car and brought in their luggage.

Fritz must not be deaf, he just doesn't speak much, if any.

The old woman stood, and told the creature where to take the luggage, then she called, "Ada," and a pudgy middle aged blond appeared. Her hair was bradded and twisted into a tight bun on the back of her head. She wore a large apron, and was carrying a long handled wooden spoon. After a brief discussion in German, she went back to the kitchen. Mandy figured she was the cook and getting instructions about lunch.

Doesn't anyone ever speak English? I feel like I'm in Germany, but I know I am just south of Washington, DC. I'd like very much to understand what is going on. This is all so strange, and I'm getting very scared.

Suddenly, the creature came in, grabbed Mandy by an arm and pulled her up; her hands still tied behind her back He pulled her to a door, opened it and dragged her stumbling down the stairway to a basement room. It was all cinderblock, painted a light blue, and sparsely furnished. Only a twin size bed, one leatherbound chair that looked fairly comfortable, a small vanity with a mirror, a bench, and a small chest of drawers. The creature untied her hands, threw her roughly into the chair, turned and rushed up the stairs locking the door behind him.

She sat and looked around the room. In a minute, Fritz returned with her suitcase and makeup kit. Then he left, locking the door behind him

The bed was made. It had a nice pillow, and the creature had put her suitcase on it. She figured her clothes from the other place were in it. The bed looked decent, but not nearly as nice she'd had at the other house. The makeup case he had put on the dresser. She looked around some more, and saw there was a wardrobe where she could put her hanging clothes, but there was no bathroom. What was she to do about that when she had to go or take a shower?

I guess I'll have to go bang on the door and yell.

After she collected her thoughts, she got up and began putting things away. She hoped lunch would be soon.

Just as she was done, the key in the lock startled her. She was surprised to see the fat man come down the basement steps. He stopped at the bottom of the stairs. She stood gaping at him.

"You should know, we are taking you to Germany tomorrow," he said.

"I thought you were taking me home."

He didn't answer, but left, locking the door again, and Mandy stood dumbfounded.

CHAPTER 9

"It turned out to be brilliant, Brenda," said Dan. "To focus on only Germans, and to think of searching for ones that only recently came to Washington, then to look for only short-term rentals. You were absolutely on target, and found them. Dietrich and Clara Schmidt. I'm astounded."

"Me, too," said Kathleen.

Brenda smiled demurely. "Thank you."

"You found them, and you barely missed them. Best of all, you found that tag from Mandy's jogging halter. Mary recognized it immediately when she saw it," Dan said.

Brenda frowned. "But they're gone, and we have no idea where."

Dan said, "Yes, that's true."

They were lunching on the massive back porch of the McLean mansion. It was not screened in as was Dan's house in Dallas, nor did it have a big porch swing.

In a few moments, Brenda said, "What if they took her to Germany?"

"What makes you say that? Why would they take her to Germany?"

"No real reason," said Brenda. "Just speculation. But if you could have seen where she was kept, Dan. Her room was *very* nice. She wasn't kept like a normal kidnapped victim. Then there's the fact they rented a big grand piano. I think they treated her well, and possibly made her continue her practicing. Then, returning the piano so quickly, I believe they just might be taking her to Germany for some strange reason."

"Everything you've said makes sense except the part about taking her to Germany," said Dan.

Yeah," said Kathleen. "I see no purpose in that. They could not expect her to perform publicly in Germany, she is too well known all over the world."

"You're right, of course," said Brenda, looking at Kathleen. "Maybe they have something else in mind. I can't imagine what, but I still have this gut feeling that they are planning to take her to Germany."

Dan thought for a minute. "Your gut feelings have been spot on so far, Brenda. I think it is worth consideration, even if you are wrong. We can't just sit around waiting for a shoe to drop."

"But," said Kathleen, "how could they take her? She would need a visa, a passport, and all sorts of papers to get out of the country and into another."

"That's right," said Brenda, "and then, would the Schmitz's use their names in booking passage, or would they choose an alias?"

"Fake papers are not too hard to come by, I have a drawer full with all kinds of aliases, as you well know, sweetheart."

"Oh, yes. I remember well," said Kathleen. "You have some with the most ridiculous names; Jack and Jill Strange, as I recall when we went to Israel last year."

Dan gave a twisted smile and said, "I have one for 'Ben Dover.'"

Brenda broke up laughing. "You're not serious."

"I'm afraid he is," said Kathleen.

***

They are taking me to Germany? He said he was taking me home. I don't understand. Maybe he meant his home.

She went to lie down on the bed. She lay on her back, staring blankly at the basement ceiling. She had to think She began to drift off into sleep, when a key unlocked the basement door, and in a moment, the maid that had met them at the door came down to the bottom step and stopped.

"Lunch is ready," she said.

The maid said was Emelia Muller, and she had immigrated to the US, in 1979 at the age of twenty-six, and found a job as a domestic in the home of a wealthy widow, Mia Becker, an older woman. Mrs. Becker lived in a mansion just outside of Woodbridge, Virginia, in a heavily wooded area that was somewhat remote and isolated. Emelia had come to America to flee an abusive husband. She was the only servant in the Becker household who was not afraid to learn to drive an American car, so she became the one Mrs. Becker would send to run errands for her. Consequently, she had learned to speak English fairly well, though she still spoke with a strong German accent.

Mandy was shocked to hear her speak English. Before the woman could turn to leave, she said, "Wait. You speak English."

She looked puzzled. "Yes, why?"

"They told me they were taking me home, then he just told me they are taking me to Germany tomorrow. I want to let my parents know I'm being taken to Germany. Would you help me?"

A loud voice from upstairs yelled, "Emelia!"

"We must go," she whispered, "come. We are coming!" she shouted back to the woman upstairs. Mandy quickly joined her, and they went upstairs.

Everyone was already seated; the old woman, the fat man and his wife, Fritz Somebody, and a place beside him where she, obviously, was to sit.

"What took so long?" asked the fat man.

"I was lying down," explained Mandy. "It took me a minute to get up."

The woman, fat man's wife, just looked at her. Then their food was served by Emelia. It was a second name she had heard mentioned at the table; Fritz, and now, Emelia, first names only. As she was serving everyone, eventually Emelia came to serve Mandy. As she served her, she surreptitiously slipped a small piece of paper and a pencil stub into her lap. Mandy immediately put a hand over them and slid them into a pocket on the skirt of her dress.

A casual conversation began, but only in German. Mandy ate slowly and quietly trying to be as invisible as possible. She could hardly contain her excitement about the paper and pencil stub, and was very anxious to see what was on the paper.

"Dietrich," said the old woman, and then she spoke in German, but Mandy caught it.

Fat man's name is Dietrich Something. Three first names now. I'm making progress.

After lunch, the creature escorted Mandy back to her cell in the basement. That is the way she thought of it; a cell, a kind of prison.

As soon as she was alone, Mandy took out her note and read it.

"I will try to help you escape tonight," was all it said.

CHAPTER 10

"Ok," said Dan. "Let's think about the possibility of the Schmidt's taking Mandy to Germany."

"I don't think they would take her by ship. It would be too complicated and take too long," said Kathleen, "they must be planning to take a plane."

"Right," said Brenda. "Just think about a flight from Dulles to Germany. That plane would be filled with Germans."

"True," said Dan.

Brenda nodded. "But if Mandy was their prisoner, how could they handle that?"

"That, my dear Brenda, is the sixty-four-thousand-dollar question," said Dan. "But another problem is *we* have no idea which airport? There are many near enough that they would not necessarily have to use Dulles."

"Well," said Brenda, "what if they *did* choose Dulles? What if they thought we wouldn't even think they might be taking her to Germany? What if choosing another airport never occurred to them? What if they were indeed planning to use Dulles."

"Mmm," said Dan. "Then we have the problem of how many flights per day there are, and which one and which day would they choose, and where in Germany would they be flying?"

"Just a suggestion, Dan," said Brenda. "I'll take a look at Dulles, just to see if anything interesting shows up. It won't hurt anything."

"Another *gut* feeling, Brenda?" said Dan.

"Yeah."

"Go for it," said Kathleen.

***

She was in bed, covers over her, pretending to be asleep in case she had any unexpected and unwanted visitors to come. She was very happy her jogging outfit had made it this far, and she was dressed in it instead of a nightgown, hoping to run away if Emelia did come to help her escape. She even had her running shoes on in bed. She was indeed ready to run away.

It was difficult to stay awake so long, but the thought of escaping helped. With no watch or clocks, she had no idea of the time when she heard someone slip a key quietly into the lock, and gently turn it.

Sure enough, it was Emilia padding barefoot down the stairs dressed in her nightgown. When she saw Mandy sit up on the side of her bed, she motioned for her to come quickly. As silently as they could, Emilia led Mandy to a back door, opened it, and let Mandy dash as fast as she could into the woods.

Emilia left the backdoor wide open, just as she had left the door to the basement wide open. Then she quickly returned to her own room and jumped into bed. No lights had been turned on, and virtually no sound made. The house continued to be very quiet.

Mandy ran flat out to the woods about thirty yards away. She had pulled back her long hair into a pony-tail, just as it was the night she was abducted. When she entered the woods the darkness slowed her. The sky was overcast. The thickness of the trees and the underbrush slowed her to a walk. Small branches lashed at her face, arms and legs; stinging and scratching her skin. If she could only see better. She had no since of direction, and was just wandering aimlessly.

*I don't know where I'm going,
and I don't know where to go.*
   After what seemed like hours,
she was still milling about in the
woods, hopelessly lost. She saw no
houses, no roads, and no way to
know which way to civilization. She
had tripped and fallen twice, scraping
her left knee. It wasn't a bad wound;
not much bleeding. Of course it was
similarly wooded around her parents'
home in Mclean, but she had never
ventured more than a few yards into
it. She began to think she would
never find her way out.

***

Mia Becker roused from her sleep,
and looked at her bedside clock. It
had big red numbers that told her it
was just after midnight. Her mouth
was so dry. She thought she must
have been sleeping with her mouth
open. She got out of bed, slipped on
a robe, and went to the kitchen for a
drink of water. On her way to the
kitchen, she passed by the door to

the basement, and was startled to see it wide open. Then she glanced into the kitchen, and saw the back door was also standing open. Hurriedly, she went down the basement stairs only to see their prisoner had escaped. She smiled.

Good. It serves them right.

She closed the door to the basement, and closed the back door, then casually got her glass of water. Then she took her time before going to her daughter's bedroom to knock on the door. It was another minute or so before the door opened a crack and a sleepy eye peeked out.

"Mother?"

"You might want to tell that pig of a husband of yours that your precious prodigy has escaped."

"What? When?"

"I have no idea, but I found the basement door wide open when I went to get a drink of water, and so was the back door. She's gone."

"Who let her out?"

"Beats me, but I'm glad she got away." They both were speaking in English.

Clara suddenly closed the door.

Some minutes later, Dietrich rushed out of the room clothed in his robe and slippers, and went to Fritz's door and went in, not bothering to knock. There was a lot of shouting, and in a few minutes Fritz ran out, and then ran out the back door. He wore blue jeans, a long sleeved sweatshirt and sneakers without sox. The long sleeves and jeans would help to ward off the whipping of the underbrush branches.

When Clara appeared again, she was in a dress and flat shoes, her hair was brushed, and her face made up. Dietrich went back in their bedroom to dress. Mia went back to bed. It wasn't her problem.

Fritz dashed into the woods. He was frantic to find her. The darkness prevailed, so it was very difficult for him to find his way through the woods, too. He had no idea which way to go, either. It seemed a futile effort, but he plunged on.

CHAPTER 11

Dietrich woke the three servant girls, and got them together in the parlor. He spoke in English.

"One of you released the girl," he shouted. "Which one of you did it?"

They were terrified of the big man. They cowered before him, but said nothing.

"Tell me," he roared, but still they were silent and shaking in fear.

"Aaaaaach!" he screamed. "I'll kill all of you if you don't speak up!"

Ada, the cook, spoke first, but in a subdued voice. "I . . . I didn't, I swear."

Addy, Mrs. Becker's personal maid, began shaking her head, "Not me," she said.

"Neither did I," said Emelia.

"One of you did! Now which one of you. You are the only ones in the house that could have! Tell me!" He was shouting at them as they sat compliant.

Dietrich decided he didn't much think the cook did it, so he grabbed the wrist of the youngest of the two, Mia's personal maid, Addy, a twenty year old German girl, and drew her close to his face.

"Are you the one?" She felt his spittle on her face they were so close. It revulsed her.

"No!" She shouted back at him. "I don't even have a key to the basement."

He shoved her back into the chair, and turned to the third girl,

Emelia, the charwoman, but before he could grab her, she shrank back and said, "I did have a key, but I lost it a week ago." She lied. She did still have her key.

He moved to tower over her, glaring at her. "Yes, *you* are the one! *You* let her go!"

"Oh, no, sir," she whined. "Why would I do such a thing?"

Mia Becker came in at that moment. She was wearing her robe over her pajamas, and house shoes.

"What is going on? Why are you shouting at my girls?"

Dietrich looked at his mother-in-law, "One of them helped the girl escape. I'm trying to find out which one." He said.

"Not all of them had keys," said Mia. She turned to the girls.

"Which one of you let her go?"

All three denied it again.

She stepped to her cook, Ada, and said, "Did you do it, Ada?"

"No ma'am. I didn't know she was gone."

Mia then turned to Addy. "Your keys, please," she said.

"I don't have a key to the basement, ma'am, remember? I couldn't have done it."

"I was asleep," said Ada, the cook.

"I was, too," said Emelia.

"Where are your keys, Emelia?"

"I lost mine last week, I was afraid to tell you, ma'am."

"You *lost* your keys?"

"Yes, ma'am. I'm so sorry. I couldn't have done it."

"Well," said Mia. "It looks as though we have a mystery. How do you know the girl didn't manage to unlock the basement door herself someway? You *don't* know, Deitrick. You can't be sure. Just forget about it. She is gone."

Dietrich fumed. He wanted to hurt somebody. Or kill them.

***

Mandy was beginning to feel her escape was futile, but then she suddenly saw a road in front of her. She could run again, so she turned to the right to run with the flow of traffic, but there was no traffic at this time of night. She again ran as fast as she could. Soon, on her left, she saw a house, but it was dark. She decided to keep running. It wasn't long till she saw a gas station, but it was closed. She spotted a pay phone outside the building, but she had no money. Then she seemed to remember that there was some way to access a line for emergencies, but she couldn't remember exactly how.

Why didn't I pay better attention?

She jogged up to the phone, and began to study it, trying to remember something about how to get accesses. She stood there fiddling with the phone, when suddenly a strong hand clamped over her mouth, and another strong arm wrapped around her body. It was Fritz. He had caught her.

When he let go of her mouth she screamed as loudly as she could. He slapped her face hard.

It made her cry. "Let me go," she protested.

"Shut your face or I will hit you with my fists."

She was stunned. He spoke in English. He was big and strong as an ox, but his voice was high and squeaky. Almost childlike. It almost made her want to laugh.

"Don't say one more word, you hear me?"

"Yes," she whispered; one word just for spite. Just then, the clouds began to part, and a three-quarter moon shone brightly.

Now it shines, thought Mandy

Fritz had a coil of rope wrapped over one shoulder and down across his body. He obviously had some sense of direction to find her so quickly, and he was well prepared. He tied her hands together securely in front of her, wrapped the rope around her waist to include both her arms, tied her and began to lead her back. He made her walk in front of him. With a bright moon, Fritz easily found the way back to the house.

When Dietrich saw Fritz bring her in, he said, "Take her back to the basement, and lock her in. You have a key. We have a flight to catch back to Germany in the morning."

"It *is* morning," said Mia as she turned and went back to her room.

Mandy still had no idea of the time, but she was sure it must be pretty close to dawn. She sat down on the side of her bed, dejected. She had almost escaped.

I'm not going to cry.

But, a tear rolled down her cheek. She got up, dressed in a short, blue nightgown with straps over her shoulders, put her jogging outfit away, and crawled back into bed. Dietrich, the fat man, said they were leaving for Germany tomorrow morning. She had to make one more attempt to let someone know. She got up and went to the wardrobe where she found the dress she had on when Emelia slipped the note to her at lunch, and the note was still in the pocket. She took it to the vanity, and with the small pencil stub she wrote her parent's phone number, and the words, "Call my parents and tell them that I'm being taken to Germany." She put the paper back in the skirt pocket; folding it carefully, she hid the dress under the mattress, leaving a small bit of fabric showing at the edge. Emelia was the one she believed most likely to tend to the room after she left. Her hope was Emelia would find the dress with the note and call her parents.

Exhausted, she climbed back in bed, and was soon asleep.

CHAPTER 12

Wednesday, September 10, 1986

Next morning, before Mandy woke, a
key slid quietly into the lock on the
basement door and turned. Silently,
Dietrich and Fritz came down the
stairs, and came to stand beside her
bed. She hadn't heard them at all,
and was deep in sleep. The two men

stood looking down on her. Her long, dark hair was loosely arrayed around her head. Her arms were on top of the covers, and bore marks where she was lashed by the branches as she rushed to get away, but they were few, and not severe. Her face was serene with her wideset eyes shut, her lips closed, her cheeks full, and with her small nose, she was a beautiful young woman to behold. Neither man moved for a moment. Both men were dressed in a suit and tie, like mismatched business men. Their dress shoes were polished, and bore rubber soles so they were quiet. Each wore a carnation on their jackets.

Dietrich slipped his right hand into the side pocket, and withdrew a syringe. Quickly, he plunged the needle into the fatty tissue on her shoulder. She immediately came awake and tried to move away from the pain, but Fritz was quicker, and held her still until the syringe was empty. She stared up at them in terror, but very soon she was once again still and quiet, and drifted back to sleep.

The two men went back upstairs, and in a few minutes were struggling to get a very lightweight casket down the steps. They placed it next to her bed. When they opened it, the inside was white, and plush. It looked comfortable. She should be fine in it for a few hours. Fritz picked her up at her shoulders as Dietrich took her feet. They laid her gently inside and closed the lid with a snap. Dietrich and Fritz had made several vents in the casket so Mandy could breath, but they were well disguised, and so would be unnoticeable to a casual observer. She would not suffocate.

It was Dietrich who had the hardest time carrying the foot of the casket as they made their way back upstairs. It was six o'clock in the morning. Their flight to Germany was to leave Dulles International at nine-twenty. They set the casket on a gurney in the livingroom. The station wagon was parked near the front door.

Clara and her mother were standing in the livingroom when they brought the casket in, Clara was dressed in black mourning attire, her mother in her normal attire, she wasn't going anywhere. She glared at them all in disapproval, but what could she do? Dietrich would not hesitate to kill her or anyone else that stood in his way. It was her daughter she could not understand. She did whatever he said even though he was a terrible man. Why didn't she leave him? Why did she marry the big fat slob in the first place. They met here in the United States, but as soon as they were married, he took her to live in Germany with him.

The three servant girls managed to keep hidden from view as they watched the proceedings from the kitchen. They were scared of the fat man and his strong accomplice, but were now very anxious for them to go away; back to Germany. They liked Mrs. Becker. She was kind and generous with them. The casket, however, was very troubling. Had they killed the young lady? They did not understand anything that was going on since Clara came with her husband and the other man. Life would be good again after those three were gone.

"She should sleep most of the way, if not all the way to Frankfurt," said Dietrich.

Mia could not help herself, "That poor girl," she said out loud.

Dietrich looked at his mother-in-law with sheer hatred.

"You know nothing," he said. "She will be better off in Germany where she belongs. Let's go, Fritz, you drive the station wagon. Clara, you sit up front with Fritz, you are the grieving mother. I am the funeral director. I will sit in the back seat with the casket. We need to be at the airport early. It takes time to make proper arrangements to ship a casket."

Clara nodded her head. She seldom spoke, but her mother was not so hesitant.

"What if she wakes up?"

"I am sure she would be scared if she wakes, and I'm also sure she would scream, but in the baggage compartment, who would hear? However, I don't think she will wake up until we have her home."

Mia was so angry with her daughter she would not even say, "Goodbye."

***

After breakfast, Dan, Kathleen, and Brenda took another mug of coffee out to the large patio behind the house to sit and make plans for the day. Of course Brenda wasn't allowed to see any manifests when she went to the airport, and it might not have made any difference if she could have. It would probably have taken a court order for even the police to see a manifest. Nevertheless, she'd tried.

As Kathleen's habit was on such occasions, she opened the conversation saying, "Ok, Sherlock, what's next?"

Dan said, "It would be useless to just go out to Dulles and watch each flight to Germany. I am afraid we are back to square one."

"We don't even know where in Germany they might go," said Brenda.

Kathleen sighed heavily. "It seems hopeless. We need some kind of break."

***

After the big station wagon drove away, Mia turned to her housekeepers and said, "Alright, ladies, let's get things back to normal, I'm going to go lie down a while."

It was indeed Emelia's job to take care of the basement room where Mandy had stayed. When she got to it, as she changed the sheets on the bed, she noticed a piece of pink fabric protruding out from under the mattress. She lifted it and found the dress Mandy had worn yesterday. Absently, she stuck her hand in each of the pockets on the skirt, and found the note. She was shocked to read it, and hurried upstairs to the kitchen phone and dialed the number. She knew her mistress was in her room and wouldn't hear.

A man's voice said, "Hello, the Lynn residence."

"Who is this?" Emelia asked in just above a whisper.

"This is Tom Lynn, who are you?"

"Emelia, I am a maid for Mrs. Mia Becker. We have been keeping a prisoner here, a young lady. She left me this number and said you were her parents. I can't talk but just a minute or I'll be caught. She wanted me to tell you her captors are taking her to Frankfurt this morning. They said she was alive, but she was in a casket, so I don't really know for sure. They just left for the airport. I have to hang up now."

***

Tom Lynn stood gaping at the phone. *Emelia? May Something . . . or Mia? Yes, Mia. Mandy may be dead? Then why would they take her body to Frankfurt? I think she must be alive."*

"Who was it on the phone, honey?"

It was Mary. He wasn't about to tell her Mandy could be dead or going to Frankfurt, Germany. Not till he was sure.

"I'm not sure who it was, sweetheart. It was just some prankster, I think, Didn't make any sense to me. Think I'll go over to Dan's a while. You want to come?"

"No, I want to stay near the phone. The FBI are no longer monitoring calls."

CHAPTER 13

Thursday, September 11, 1986

It was almost 9 a.m. when Tom pulled to a stop in front of Dan's house. He rang the doorbell, and in a moment, Dan was opening the door.

"Hi, Tom. What brings you over this morning? Come in, my friend, and have some coffee with us."

"Don't mind if I do, thanks. I just got a strange phone call I'd like to tell you about."

"Sure, we'll pick you up a mug on our way out. Kathleen and Brenda are out back on the patio, and we were discussing Mandy's kidnapping."

When they were settled, Dan said, "Tell us about your strange phone call, Tom."

When he finished telling about it, Dan said, "I think we'd better get out to Dulles and watch for a casket being loaded on a plane. Come on, Brenda. You, too, sweetheart."

As a quick afterthought, he added, "Come with us, Tom."

They all piled into Dan's nine passenger station wagon and left.

When they got to Dulles and went into the terminal Dan began looking for a baggage handler. When he found one, he asked if a casket had been loaded on a flight to

Germany, and he told him one had been on a flight to Frankfurt earlier that morning.

He turned to Kathleen, and said, "Looks like I have to fly to Frankfurt, sweetheart. I'm going back to the car to get my travel bag. I'll take the next flight out to Frankfurt."

He ran out to his car. When he returned, he handed Kathleen the car keys. "Take everyone back, honey." He kissed her goodbye and went to buy his ticket. Thankfully, he always carried a suitcase in his car with clothes and all the documents he would need to travel anywhere at any time.

***

Kathleen drove; Brenda by her side, and Tom in the back. The day was beautiful in Virginia with the sun shining brightly, and everything still green and plush. Leaves would be turning soon, however, and the beautiful fall colors would be glorious again in Virginia. No one was paying any attention to mother nature. They were all deeply troubled by the turn of events in Mandy's kidnapping. Kathleen looked at Tom in the back seat through the rearview mirror. His head was back, resting. His eyes were closed, and she could see tears slowly seeping down his cheeks. The frown on his face told her he was deep in thought.

She focused on the road again. Tom's head came forward; his chin resting on his chest. He said softly, but had a hard time getting the words out, "We aren't even sure she is still alive."

"I know," said Kathleen with as much empathy as she could give.

Brenda spoke up, "I believe she *is* alive, Tom, and I believe she will be when they land in Frankfurt. She's going to be fine. I really believe it."

He didn't respond. Brenda continued, "We need to help Dan in Germany, Tom, think hard. Try to remember the names your caller mentioned. It is vital to help us find her. You said Emelia called, try to remember her last name."

His forehead furrowed as he thought, "The caller didn't tell me her last name, only her first; Emelia, but she did have a German accent."

"Great, Tom. That's great. We know the names of the pair that took her, Dietrich and Clara Schmidt, and we know the name of the woman Emelia mentioned. You said her first name was Mia, right?"

"Hmmm," said Tom. "Yes, that was a name she mentioned."

"Try to remember her last name."

"B, it started with a b, I think."

"Good," urged Brenda.

"Baker... no... Becker! It was Mia Becker."

"Wonderful, Tom. I can find her. When I do, we will go talk to her."

Kathleen looked at Brenda out of the corner of her eyes, "Good work, Brenda."

"Yes, thank you," she said, "and perhaps what we learn from Mia

Becker will help Dan to find them in Germany."

"Now I am excited," said Kathleen.

"Tom, you really came through, my friend. Thanks for your help," said Brenda.

"It's *my* daughter," he said, "it's important."

"Of course it's important," said Kathleen, "it's her life we're talking about, and now we have a real lead, thanks to you."

They sped back to Goodwoods as fast as they could, and when they stopped, Brenda jumped out of the car, went to Dan's study to begin her search for Mia Becker. Kathleen then drove Tom back to his house to drop him off.

***

Dan had checked his bags, but kept his attaché with him as he entered the big 747. Of course, he could not take his Glock, but he'd called ahead to make arrangements in Frankfort for a gun to be waiting for him at the hotel desk.

He found his first class seat, and placed his attaché in the overhead compartment, then settled in for takeoff. He glanced around the first class section. Mostly Germans, he thought as he heard them in conversation.

The huge aircraft climbed steeply into an azure blue sky. Below, he would pass over Goodwoods, and then the capital city of the nation giving him a sense of *déjà vu.* It was not that long ago that he and Kathleen left the country for Paris. Fond memories flooded his mind about their adventure that brought them together and to fall in love.

He glanced out the window to see in the distance a streak of vapor from a jet fighter that was only a speck of gleaming silver.

He thought about Mandy in a similar plane miles ahead. He knew Brenda would find something of substance soon. When he landed in

Frankfurt, he would call her after he checked in to his hotel.

A stewardess smiled pleasantly at him. She nodded and came to his seat. He spoke first. "Schwarzer kaffee bitte." He decided to try out his German.

"Of course, sir," she said in broken English. She was a German girl, but her accent was not much at all. I know you are American. I speak English."

"And very well."

"Thank you, sir. I will be right back."

In minutes, she returned with his drink, "Here you are, sir. Black coffee."

"Thanks." Dan took the coffee from the attractive young girl with the lovely eyes. There was a time he might have made flirted with her, but now he was a happily married man with a child on the way.

It would be hours before they would touch down in the fifth largest city in Germany.

CHAPTER 14

Brenda found the address and phone number for Mia Becker, and rushed out of Dan's study to find Kathleen. Not bothering to call first, the two women dashed out to the station wagon and sped off. When they finally came upon the right address, they were both surprised to see the nice big house in a heavily wooded area in a section of Woodbridge similar to Dan and Kathleen's place in McLean. It was nearing lunchtime, but Kathleen proceeded up the long driveway to the house. Near the house, the driveway divided. Straight ahead, it went to a garage, but the turn left went along the front of the house. Kathleen stopped near the front door. The porch ran the width of the house. Actually, it was more of a veranda than a porch. The two women got out, and went to ring the doorbell. A short, heavyset young woman in her thirties answered the door.

"Yes?"

Kathleen took the lead, "Hello. Is this the home of Mrs. Mia Becker?"

"Yes. May I ask who is calling?"

"I am Kathleen Good, and this is my friend, Brenda White. We are private investigators." She handed the woman one of Dan's business cards.

Emelia frowned. She was surprised, but asked, "What is this about?"

"Our business is with Mrs. Becker. It is confidential."

She stared at the card a moment, then said, "Please, come in. Wait here in the foyer." She quickly walked away. The business card had scared her. Who were these women, and why did they insist on seeing her mistress?

"Wow!" said Brenda. Look at this place."

"Very impressive," Kathleen agreed.

"This lady is rich."

Mrs. Becker was in the kitchen, talking to Ada, the cook. When she saw Emelia, she turned toward her. "What is it Emelia?"

"You have visitors, ma'am. They are in the foyer."

"Well," she said, "what do they want?"

"They said it was confidential, and they handed me this card." She handed the card to her.

When she read the card, it greatly disturbed her. "Private investigators? What on earth could they possibly want from me?" She slipped the business card in a pocket.

"Shall I tell them you are coming?"

"No. Tell them I don't want to see
them. Tell them to go away."

"Yes, ma'am," said Emelia and left.

The two visitors were still standing in the foyer. Emelia said, "My mistress
said she will not see you, and you must go
away."

"Shall we tell the FBI about her? They will be very interested she has held a kidnap victim hostage in this house. Would she rather see the FBI than us?"

Emelia's jaw dropped, and she clamped both hands over her mouth, turned and fled. She ran back to her mistress, "Mrs. Becker," she exclaimed. They threated to tell the FBI about you; I think you need to talk to them."

That really shook her. "The FBI? Go tell them I'm coming. Have them go into the parlor."

Upon her return, she said, "My mistress will see you in the parlor. Follow me, please."

No sooner had they sat down, than Mrs. Becker entered. Kathleen and Brenda were both surprised to see she was an older woman. She looked very much like what a German matron might look like. Conservatively dressed in a dark, short sleeved green blouse and dark slacks with flat shoes, she did not greet them, but sat across from them, crossed her ankles, folded her hands in her lap and said, "Now, what is all this nonsense about the FBI? I have no idea what you are talking about."

They could detect a slight German accent. Brenda spoke first, "Oh, I think you do, Mrs. Becker. A young lady, named Amanda Lynn was kidnapped and kept in this house and was smuggled to Frankfurt in a casket this morning."

Now Mrs. Becker's jaw dropped, and she began to cry. She wept bitterly with her hands over her face. It was some time before she could gain her composure.

Softly, she said, "I am so ashamed."

Kathleen spoke gently to her, "Tell us about it, please. Her parents want her back."

With a deep sigh, she said, "Of course they do. I felt sorry for the young lady. I was very angry at them when they called and told what they wanted me to do for them.

"It was Dietrich. Deitrick is such a brute and a fool. It was he and his cousin, Fritz, that did the kidnapping. My daughter, Clara, was not directly involved. She was forced to become his accomplice. They drugged the girl and put her in a casket. He said she would sleep until they landed in Frankfurt. I tried not to let him keep the poor girl in my basement, but he threatened me. He has a gun, you see. Please don't report me to the FBI, I would surely go to prison for something I had no real control over. I am too old to go to prison," and she began to cry again, heavily.

Brenda was sympathetic, "It is actually against the law for us *not* to report you, Mrs. Becker, but if you fully cooperate with us, we will do our best to protect you."

She resigned herself. "Alright," she said, "what do you want to know?"

Brenda took a writing pad and pen from her purse, and said, "Our colleague is on his way to Frankford as we speak, and we know your daughter and son-in-law are also on their way there, so we need to tell our colleague where to find them in Frankfort. What is their name and address?"

"I'll have to go get my address book. Just a minute." She got up and left the room.

When she returned, she handed a slip of paper to Brenda. "I wrote their name and address down for you; and the phone number."

"Thank you," said Brenda. She looked at it and said, "Dietrich Stroheim? the great conductor of the Frankfort Symphony Orchestra?" she was shocked. I can't believe he would kidnap anyone."

"You don't know him. I was not surprised at all, just disgusted with the big slob. I can't believe my daughter married him.

"I never even knew the girl's name," she said as she sat back down.

"Amanda is the daughter of Tom and Mary Lynn, next door neighbors of me and my husband," said Kathleen, "that is how we got involved. My husband is Dan Good, owner of Good Investigators, a private detective agency. Mandy is a world famous concert pianist. Did you know that?"

"No. I had no idea. I was told nothing."

"Yes. She was a child prodigy; made her debut at age thirteen."

Brenda asked, "Do you know why they kidnapped her? They have never asked for ransom, they never seemed to have abused her, but they rented a large grand piano for her. Kept her in a lovely room. What do they want with her, and why have they taken her to Germany?"

Mrs. Becker shook her head, "I only know they were holding her against her will. I can't imagine why they would take her to Germany. She did escape from here last night."

This surprised Kathleen, "She escaped?"

"Yes, but Fritz found her before she could get away."

"I am amazed she would try, good for her."

"I was so disappointed she didn't get away."

"Well," said Kathleen standing up, "we must be leaving. Thank you Mrs. Becker. This will be a great help to our colleague in finding her."

Mrs. Becker and Brenda stood, and
they all walked to the front door and said their goodbyes.

Mia Becker watched them drive off,
then went back in the house and to her
room. She closed the door. She knew
their flight had not yet reached Frankfurt,
but she picked up the telephone and placed a transatlantic call to Frankfurt. When she heard someone answer, she had a short conversation in German, and hung up.

She is *my daughter.*

CHAPTER 15

Dan had not been in Frankfort since he was in the CIA. His German was not so good now, but he thought it was passable.

They'd been in the air about 9 hours. Meals had been tolerable, but the inflight movie was one he and Kathleen had seen, so he went up to the lounge. He had no reason to go, but he needed to stretch his legs.

Another attractive stewardess asked him if she could get him a drink. She spoke to him in German. He didn't want any more caffeine, so he told her, "Nothing, thank you."

A man seated nearby heard him speak in English to the stewardess, so said,
"You are American, I hear." He had a German accent, but his English was good.

"I am," he answered.

"Ach. I am American, too, but not by birth; immigration." He moved closer to Dan. Dan looked him over. He was dressed
in a suit and tie; stocky, and about mid-
fifties, he thought.

The man said, "Frankfurt was my
birthplace, and I am going to visit what's
left of my family. Haven't seen them for years"

"You're traveling alone?"

"Yes. My wife, an American, stayed with our three children who are in school. And, you? You also are traveling alone?"

Dan shifted in his seat to be more toward his traveling companion. "I am. I am on a business trip. My wife is expecting our first child, and didn't think it wise to come along."

"Congratulations. My name is Henrik Schmidt." He offered his hand to shake. Dan took it, thought startled at the name, "I'm Good, Dan Good. Happy to meet you, Mr. Schmidt."

"Likewise," said the man.

Dan maintained a bland expression on his face, and said, "Your name is Schmidt? What a coincidence. I am going to Frankfurt to try to locate a man named, Dietrich Schmidt, he wouldn't, by chance, be one of your kin, would he?"

"I'm sorry, but no, he is not a relative, so far as I know."

"I didn't think so, that would be too much of a coincidence."

They chatted for a while, but Dan never discussed what his business was in Frankfurt. Finally, Dan excused himself and went back to his seat in first class. He sat in the semidarkness, leaned back as far as was possible without disturbing the person in the seat behind him, and slept.

***

It was getting dark in Frankfurt when Dietrich quickly arranged for the casket containing Mandy to be transferred into the waiting station wagon; his own, this time. Once he was alone in the back with the casket, and they were on their way, he opened it to find Mandy waking from her long sleep. Fritz helped her get out. She was groggy and disoriented, so she gave little struggle or protest. Dietrich helped her into the backseat and sat with her as Fritz got into the front passenger seat. Then, Clara got into the back seat with Dietrich and Mandy. Dietrich's chauffeur had met them with the car and drove them away.

"Everything went just as planned," said Dietrich with great satisfaction."

"You are such a genius," said Clara, but he seemed not to notice her comment dripped with sarcasm.

***

When the big 747 landed, Dan took a taxi to the Steigenberger hotel, and checked in. He quickly settled into his suite, and called overseas to his home. The time difference was about seven hours, so it was just after lunch at Goodwoods. He was pleased that
Kathleen answered on the third ring.

"Hello, sweetheart. I miss you terribly."

"I miss you, too, honey. I figured you would call when you got settled in your hotel. You'll be happy to know we have an address for you."

"Great! Brenda is amazing."

"Yes, she is. She found the people that called Tom. We went to see a woman named, Mia Becker way out in Woodbridge. She is the mother of Clara. They kept Mandy in the basement of her house, and, guess what... Mandy escaped. But they caught her. Anyway, honey, here is their address." She read it to him and the phone number, and they chatted for a while. It would be tomorrow before he would try to find the address.

CHAPTER 16

Friday, September 12, 1986

Dan slept till about six the next morning, quickly got up and got ready to go. He skipped breakfast; he was so anxious to find Mandy. He hurried down to the lobby and out the front door into a bright morning sun, a slight breeze caressed his face. People were rushing everywhere.

There were people from all different corners of the world. Frankfort was, as Americans might say, a melting pot. He could not suppress his admiration of the great city, the financial capital of Germany, if not the world. Money and banking were the chief products here, but he was looking for a kidnapper.

There was only one cab out front at the moment, so he got in and told the driver the address. The driver did not speak English, but Dan's German was good enough. The driver told him the address was out in the countryside outside of town. He told the driver to alert him before he
reached the address. He wanted to walk to
the house.

Dan enjoyed the beautiful landscape
of the German countryside. It wasn't long
until the driver pulled to the side of the road and stopped. He turned toward Dan and said in German,

"Look up there on the top of that hill. That is the address you seek."

The house was huge, the front double
doors were oversized and made of heavy wood and iron; they looked like they had been taken from some medieval castle. It sat on the top of a small hill on about three acres of land. It was surrounded by a nice setting of trees, shrubbery and a great lawn, all carefully and beautifully landscaped. A house of wealth. He would approach through the heavy shrubbery that began at roadside, and climbed up on the right side of the lawn to the house. He could not be seen approaching the house from there.

"Thank you," answered Dan in German, and paid his fare. Then he carefully made his way through the virtual forest up to the house, and quickly walked up to the front door to ring the bell.

In a few moments, the door was opened by a butler in livery.

Of course, Dan did not expect this butler to speak English, so he said, in German, "I want to see Mr. Schmidt, please."

The butler replied, "There is no one here by that name. You have the wrong address." He tried to shut the door in Dan's face so he stuck one of size thirteen shoes in to stop the door.

"Wait!"

But the butler left the front door ajar, and continued to walk away.

"If you don't leave immediately, I am calling the police."

Dan closed the door, and walked quickly out of sight back into the thick shrubbery. He certainly did not want to involve the Frankfurt police; they would not approve of an American private investigator working in their country. They would surely take his case away for themselves, he thought. Perhaps that is what he should do – go to the police and tell them about the kidnapping, and let them take over. No, it was his job.

He was doing this for his neighbor and friend.

Carefully secluded, he watched to see if the police came. After almost a half hour, they had not come. He was certain the Schmidt's had returned. He decided to circle around to the back of the house. He still wanted not to be seen, so he was careful to sneak into position to see the back of the house. There was a large unattached garage, and he could walk right up to it without being spotted. The garage could house about four, maybe five cars, and there appeared to be an upstairs apartment above. The stars to the apartment were on the side of the garage
that were not visible from the house. How lucky was that?

First, he checked out the garage through a side window, There was only one empty space for a car. Then he went up the stairs, and there were two small windows that were covered with drapes so he could not see inside.

Bummer.

Nothing to do but leave. When he got back to ground level, he peeked around to look at the back of the house again. Everything was quiet, but just then a young man came out the back door to head for the garage. He was a small man who appeared to be in his early twenties. Perhaps he was going to take a car somewhere, of perhaps he just had some errand. Dan decided to take a chance, and quickly came around the garage to grab him with one long arm and cover his mouth with the other. Dan was so big it was nothing for him to take him around an out of sight of the house.

He said in German, "Don't make a sound or I will break your scrawny neck, understand?" The young man nodded; his eyes wide with terror.

"Tell me if Mr. Schmidt has returned yet."

He shook his head, "I don't know anyone named Schmidt." He said nothing more.

"What do you mean, you don't know anyone named Schmidt? Isn't this his home?"

"No, sir. There is nobody named Schmidt living here."

Dan was puzzled. "If he doesn't live here, who does?"

The young man said, "Maestro Sondheim."

"The symphony conductor? Alright," said Dan. "I'm going to let you go, but I'm going to make sure you don't tell anybody about me for a while." Dan hit him in a way that he would be unconscious for a good while. Then he had to find a way to get back to his hotel, and realized he would have to hitchhike.

***

Unknown to Dan, Dietrich also had another house closer to town, and that is where he hade gone.

"Come, Fritz," said Dietrich. "let's talk."

They went into Dietrich's study, and he closed the door.

"We have a problem. My mother-in-
law, Mia, called Clara, and told her some
women came to see her. They knew almost everything, and she broke down and admitted to everything, the stupid woman. Then they told her that a colleague of theirs was on his way here. The women had given Mia, a business card from a private investigating service called, Good Investigators. The man's name on the card was, Dan Good. I can't imagine how they found out about us, and so quickly. We must do something about him, this Dan Good."

"It must have been the stranger that just came to the door at your country house. Franz called to tell me of a giant of a man that came few minutes ago. Leave him to me," said Fritz. "I'll find this Dan Good, and I will take care of him. I know a few guys."

Fritz Weise went to his room, picked up the telephone to make a call. Then he went to the garage, took the Audi convertible, and drove away.

CHAPTER 17

It was lunchtime by the time Dan got back to his hotel. He ordered a meal to be sent up to his suite, and called home.

Alice Stevens, his house manager, answered.

"Good residence."

"Hi, Alice, it's Dan. Is Kathleen or Brenda handy?"

"They both happen to be standing right here. Let me give you Kathleen."

Just before Kathleen answered, Dan heard her tell Brenda to go pick up an
extension. "Hi, sweetheart," she said. "Brenda is on the extension."

"Great. Hi, to you both. I just wanted to tell you I went to the address you gave me, Brenda, but their butler said I had the wrong address, I wanted to check if I got it wrong." He read the address back to them."

"No,," said Brenda, you got it right."

"That is very puzzling," said Dan. Something is wrong."

Brenda frowned as she thought things over. Then she said, "Perhaps Mrs. Becker called to warn them you were coming, so they lied to you."

"Yeah. That's possible, I guess. Why don't you two go see Mrs. Becker again? See if you can shake her tree a little harder for me."

"Sure, sweetie," said Kathleen. We can do that, can't we Brenda?"

"Absolutely. Now I'm going to hang
up and let you two talk."

"Wait, Brenda. I just had a thought. Perhaps you might do a little background check on Mia Becker too. Could you do that?"

"It's getting late here, Dan. Remember we have about a big time difference. I don't think I can do anything tonight, but I will the first thing in the morning."

"Ok, call me when you have something."

"Sure. Now I'll get off the line so you two can talk all you want."

Dan and Kathleen talked for nearly an hour. When he hung up, he had nothing to do the rest of the afternoon but sit around and wait. Then the night would be before him. They wouldn't talk to Mrs. Becker again till tomorrow morning, their time. There were too many hours for Dan to do nothing. He was restless, and felt there must be something he

could do. Then, an idea came to
mind.

***

Johan Weber was seated in a dark
corner of the restaurant when Fritz
walked in. With
him were three other large men. Fritz
didn't
Know any of them.

"Johan," said Fritz, nodding in
greeting.

"Fritz," he responded, then he
introduced the three others,
Hermann,
Dieter, and Sebastian. You said you
needed muscle."

"Yes," agreed Fritz. "The guy is
a giant. Thanks for coming."

"They are more than just
muscle," said Johan, "Sebastian is
also a demolition expert. Dieter was
a professional boxer, and Hermann is
an expert sniper. Of course you
know my skills."

"Great," said Fritz. He turned
and grabbed a chair from nearby, and

pulled it up to sit at their table. "Now let me tell you what we need you to do."

He explained the situation with Dan Good, and they exchanged ideas and made suggestions. They talked for more than an hour.

Finally, Dieter said, "But we don't know where he is right now, right?"

"He is probably in some hotel, but we have lots of hotels," said Fritz.

"Well," said Johan, "I think we can
find his hotel, and we have a plan now. We can get ready for him."

***

Tom saw his wife huddled in a ball in the
corner of the livingroom couch, wrapped up in herself as if she was trying to withdraw from the world around her. He had tried to draw her out of herself, but so far had not been much help or comfort to her. It hurt him deeply to see her suffering, but

he had little to offer by way of encouragement. To have your only child kidnapped was beyond cruelty.

Mary had managed to stretch the long telephone cord to the coffee table, and she was sitting on the edge of the couch staring at the phone, willing it to ring to tell her Mandy was alive and well, and coming home.

Tom had not told her that her kidnappers had taken her to Germany yet. He was afraid it would kill her, and he loved her too much. She was still a beautiful woman at the age of fifty-nine. She had a fine figure, and a lovely face. Hardly any gray at all in her dark red hair. He was sixty-two, and they had been married fifty years last October. Mandy had come to them late in life, and that made her all the more precious to them.

He got up from his easy chair and went to sit by her on the couch. He took her hand and said, "Sweetheart, Mandy has been taken to Frankfurt, Germany. Dan is there now, and he has the address of the

kidnappers. He knows their names.
He will
get her and bring her home soon."

   She didn't look up. "Oh, Tom,"
she
said, and began to cry again.

   "Don't cry, darling. We know
she is
alive and she's been allowed to
practice piano every day. That is
something."

   She sniffled, and began, with
some effort, to stop crying.

   "I know," she finally said. "Dan
and Kathleen have been wonderful,
and I *do, so* appreciate their help.
But, I miss her so much. I hated
when she moved to her own place, I
loved hearing her play every day, and
she has been such a sweet daughter,
and I am so proud of her. I just can't
understand why someone would
kidnap her! Why? What could they
possibly want her? What do they
want from us?"

   "I have no idea, sweetheart."

   "What if we went to Frankfurt,
Tom? It would be better than just

sitting around here moping. We would be closer to Mandy, and when Dan rescues her, we would be right there to greet her. We could fly home with her."

"But, honey, what if he finds her before we can get there? It's about seven thousand miles to Frankfurt."

"I don't think he will. I think we have plenty of time. Oh, Tom, please."

"Alright, sweetheart. If that would make you happy."

It took them a while to pack and get
their passports and other documents together. When ready, it was very late when they went to Dulles and took the "red eye" to Frankfurt.

CHAPTER 18

Saturday, September 13, 1986

"Let me get this straight, Mr. Good," said the middle-aged attaché as he leaned back in his chair. "You want to find a man named Dietrich Schmidt, but you went to his home and was told you had a wrong address, correct?"

Dan saw the bemused expression on his face, and realized this might have been a mistake.

"Actually," Dan said awkwardly, "I am just here on business, and my neighbor back home asked if I would look them up for him while I was here. I promised I would. They knew each other some time ago. I was wondering if he might have moved."

"Didn't your friend tell exactly where to find him? He should know. Did he give you a wrong address?"

Dan considered the medium-level diplomat's question. Certainly Tom should have known, but of course, Tom didn't know anything. It wasn't good to lie, but he didn't know what else to do.

"I suppose there are several Dietrich Schmidt's in Frankfurt, and many others throughout Germany."

The attaché stood and stretched and tried unsuccessfully to stifle a yawn. He was bulky and stood just over six feet tall. He was neatly dressed in a business suit and tie. His brogans were highly polished.

"I'll see what I can find for you," he said, and walked out of his office. It wasn't very long till he returned with a sheet of paper in his hand which he handed to Dan.

"It so happens there are six Dietrich Schmidt's in Frankfurt alone.

Dan stood, "Thank you Mr. Fredricks. I'll be on my way."

The attaché smiled and shrugged as if he had solved a major scientific equation. "Good luck," he said.

Dan took the list, and when he got a cab, he gave the river the list. He looked the list over, and said, speaking German, "one of theses addresses is a home for the aged, I will take you to the others."

"Thank you," said Dan, and he sat back in his seat.

At the second address, he found that Dietrich was a teenager. At the third address, this one looked promising, but after a short interview, Dan knew he could not have been

Mandy's kidnapper. At the next address was a paraplegic in a wheelchair. The fifth and sixth also didn't
pan out, so Dan went back to his hotel, frustrated.

***

Mandy had no idea who the fat man was, except his name was Dietrich Something. She was shown through the palatial mansion from top to bottom upon her arrival. There were no bars on any windows. Maybe she could escape. How
could they stop her? Who would stop her?
She would find a way.

It was an immaculate house with many rooms and many servants. These
people who abducted her were rich.

Of course there was a piano room all its own. It had a huge nine foot Bosendorfer. Were they going to make her continue to practice her pieces? What was in store for her, she wondered? It didn't make any sense.

Finally, they showed her the bedroom that would be hers. It was bigger than her whole apartment in DC. It was *like* an apartment, except without a kitchen. There was a large seating area, a small eating table with two chairs, a large bedroom area, and a big bathroom. There was also a lock on her door, so likely she would spend most of her time locked in her room. Though her room had two nice large windows without bars, it was on the third floor. How indeed would she escape? She must find a way to get away, or at least get access to one of the many telephones she'd noticed throughout the house.

***

The woman was seventh in line behind Tom and Mary Lynn, but, of course, they didn't knew each other. When the woman finally got to the counter, she asked to get on the next flight to Frankfurt, Germany. When asked her name, she said, "Mia Becker."

CHAPTER 19

Sunday, September 14, 1986

Kathleen awoke to thunder, and turned over to look at the bedside clock. It was 9:40 a.m. She had overslept, so she checked, and found she had forgotten to set her alarm. She jumped out of bed and ran to the bathroom to shower and get ready.

When she entered the kitchen, Brenda was sitting in the breakfast nook.

"Good morning, Kathleen, I made coffee, and Alice made French toast for breakfast. Everyone has already eaten, but you. Heat some up, and get your coffee, I have things to tell you.".".

"Wonderful, Brenda. Good morning to you; I suppose the thunder woke you, too?"

"Yes, it looks like today is going to be rainy and dark."

"I think we should head right over to Mia. Becker's as soon as we can," said Kathleen. "Dan needs to know what we learn pretty soon."

"Actually, we may not need to go at all. I've already started looking into Mia Becker's past. Want to know what I found?"

Kathleen sat with her breakfast and coffee. "I sure do."

"Well," she said, "Mia was born in Frankfurt, and married Felix

Becker, a German industrialist. Not happy in Germany, she and her husband came to America where she gave birth to Clara, so Clara is actually an American citizen. Felix died of cancer, then Clara, at age fifteen, got knocked up and had a baby girl by none other than Dietrich Stroheim when he was a young piano prodigy on tour in the US. Clara's baby was adopted soon after birth by Tom and Mary Lynn. Later, when Clara reached the age of twenty-three, she met Dietrich again when he was again on tour in the States, and married him. Dietrich was ten years older than she, and they moved to Frankfurt."

"Wow," said Kathleen. "That's incredible. Dietrich Stroheim, the famous symphony conductor." I must call Dan. He has the wrong name. What time is it in Frankfurt?"

Brenda looked at her watch. "2:49 in the afternoon."

Kathleen called, and told him what Brenda had learned in her research. Dan was shocked to learn Dietrich's real name.

"I had no idea who Mandy's birth
parents were. No wonder I couldn't find him. I'm astounded that he is who kidnapped Mandy. That is why she was kidnapped. She is actually the daughter of Dietrich and Clara Stroheim."

"Yes," said Kathleen, "but why would they not rather have tried to negotiate some
kind of joint custody with Tom and Mary?"

It was a conference call, so Brenda interjected, "Maybe they did not want to share custody. Maybe they wanted Mandy back for themselves permanently. Maybe they thought Tom and Mary might not have wanted to share custody with them since they raised her as their own."

"Yeah. That's possible," said Kathleen.

"The Lynn's might not even want to let them have visiting rights," said Brenda. "Who knows?"

"So they just kidnapped her. That was dumb," said Dan. "Kidnapping is a felony here and everywhere."

"And, why do they want her?"

"They must have something in mind," said Dan. "Dietrich is certainly a world renown symphony conductor. He's come to Dallas several times; I've seen him, though it has been a while. I found he has two other homes; one in Paris, and a second home in Frankfurt. Thank you ladies, I appreciate the information."

When they ended their call, Dan made arrangements with the hotel's Concierge for a rental car. He took the elevator down to the lobby.

***

When the big plane landed in Frankfurt,

and began disgorging its passengers: among them were Mia Becker and Tom and Mary Lynn. They went their separate ways, for they didn't know each other.

Mia Becker took a cab to the home of her daughter and son-in-law; the very address she had given to Kathleen and Brenda.

The Lynn's, at random, selected the
Steigenberger Hotel, not knowing that was where Dan was staying, and took a waiting taxi at the airport.

On the drive to the hotel, Mary sighed, "I wonder how Mandy is coping."

"Well," said Tom, "you know how self-sufficient and independent she has always been. I expect she is holding her own very well. She has never been one to trifle with."

"That's true, I am still very worried."

"I know you are, sweetheart. I am,
too. I just don't know what more we can do.

I really believe that Dan will find her soon and bring her back to us."

"Of course he will," she agreed, but in her heart, she still harbored doubts.

CHAPTER 20

The air was cool, but the bright sun made the day pleasant for residents and tourists that hurried along the sidewalk that passes the entrance to the Steigenberger Hotel. The rays of the sun bounced off the waters of the nearby Main (pronounced *mine*) River, a tributary of the Reign River that snakes its way through Frankfurt.

One man wasn't the slightest impressed with the pleasant September day. His name was Hermann Schulz, sniper extraordinaire, and friend of Fritz Weiss. He stood at a window on the fourth floor of an office building diagonally across from the entrance to the Steigenberger Hotel. He was set up on a landing of a stairwell with a window, hoping he would not be

discovered while he was there. He
watched through binoculars at those
going in and coming out of the hotel,
his face was pallid, his sharp features
drawn taut, He was a large,
powerfully built man with a bit of
premature gray strands in his raven
hair. He was watching to see if Dan
Good would come out of the hotel.
He kept refocusing his binoculars,
cursing under his breath,
cursing the swift movements of the
masses below. His tired eyes were
the result of too little sleep and too
much drinking. Still, he had a job he
had to do. He was in his early
thirties. The excitement of a kill
thrilled him. He was eager, but calm.
     No one else was in the stairwell.
All was very silent. His sniper setup
was ready, so he took position, looked
through the scope and waited. The
scope was better than his binoculars,
and the high-powered rifle was
calibrated for the distance could
easily kill. He had done this often
before while in the German army, but

he'd been dishonorably discharged recently for disorderly conduct.

Fritz had told him the man he was looking for was extremely tall; six-foot-nine, and had thick black curly hair, and he would likely be wearing a business suit.

There! There he was, coming out of the hotel. The wait had been very short. With careful aim, he pulled the trigger, but in that brief moment, the tall man was jostled by passing pedestrians. He missed, and as he tried for a second quick shot, the flashing of sunlight off a passing car blinded him, and he missed again. His effort had been wasted. The man was gone. He gathered his equipment, packed it away, and left. He did not want to tell Fritz he had failed, but just because he had missed the first time didn't mean he would miss the next time he had an opportunity. He could do this, it was just a matter of when and where.

***

Dan Good had not heard the crack of rifle
fire echoing through the canyon of tall buildings because the shooter had used a silencer. An old man suddenly fell against him, and dropped to the sidewalk. Blood had spattered as his head was nearly blown away. A nearby window suddenly shattered, scattering shards of glass everywhere.

Someone is shooting..

Dan ducked quickly behind a car parked at the curb. Was it him they were shooting at, or someone else? Who knew he was here, and knew which hotel he was in?

There were no more shots it seemed, so Dan turned and ran into the hotel and up the stairs to his rooms. Blood spatter was on him and his suit. He had to shower and change clothes.

As he entered his rooms, he cracked his head on the top of the doorway. He forgot that door jams were only six-feet- eight inches, and he was six-nine. He always ducked a bit as he went from room to room, but this was one of the rare times he forgot. He didn't hesitate a moment, but quickly showered and changed into clean clothes. Then he went down to Oscar's, the Steinberger's fine restaurant. He did not want to be questioned by the police when they came to the crime scene of the dead man on the sidewalk outside.

After he was seated, he ordered black coffee. He would wait to drive out to the Stroheim's other home. He needed to think things through again. If someone was trying to kill him, he felt sure Stroheim would be behind it. He had to be more careful. The shooter had failed, but there could be other attempts awaiting him. Stroheim did not want Mandy taken from him and Clara. She was their daughter, and they had brazenly kidnapped her.

It did not take Dan long to devise a new plan. There were things he would need that he'd not expected.

He knew exactly where. The Frankfurt Main Hauptbahnhof.

Fortunately, he had been assigned to Frankfurt for a short time when he worked for the CIA, so he knew exactly what he wanted and where he could get it.

He knew counter-strategy well, and was a trained springer of unexpected traps and unanticipated death. He was, of course, a different man now, and despised the awful things he'd done in the CIA; the killings. His mind was suddenly trapped in a memory of the past.

He waited in the darkness, eyes sharp, ears
listening intently for the approach of his targets. His orders were to kill them all. He was just an instrument; he'd been conditioned to kill without hesitation. He lifted his gun. His hands were covered in latex gloves.

He saw his victims through the green night vision goggles. It was time to strike.

"No," he said out loud. "That's not who I am anymore." His work now was not so violent, nonetheless, he still had that kind of knowledge and skill from his past.

He paid his bill, left the restaurant, picked up his rental car to drive the short distance to the seedy side of Frankfurt. After parking, he made his way along the street.

As he entered the building, the heavy wooden door shut behind him. There's a smell that permeates old buildings, a taint of decay, mustiness, like dirty socks and dirty dishes, and old cats. He started up the narrow staircase, annoyed by the smell and the creaking of the dilapidated stairway. At the top of the stairs was a closed door. It was unlocked, so he stepped inside. The room reeked of cigarette smoke, the tables were old and scarred, the windows were covered in musty yellow blinds, and the smell of beer was strong, he closed the door behind him. The man behind a small table was the same man he'd done business with many years ago. He was older now, but he smiled when he saw Dan; a smile of recognition. Dan told him the things he needed, and the man left the room. After some time, he returned with a large, heavy, cloth sack, and handed it to Dan who went through it to be sure it was all exactly what he wanted. He paid the man and left. What he bought cost him three times what it would have cost when he was here last.

He drove back to his hotel rooms and set all his new toys on the eating table. Then he began putting them where he wanted them for later use. Now, he felt ready for any eventuality.

The rumble in his tummy told him it was lunchtime, and he decided he would just eat a quick lunch at Oscar's downstairs.

When he entered, Dan was shocked to see Tom and Mary just being seated in the restaurant. He almost didn't recognize them. He hadn't expected to see them in Frankfurt.

He went directly to them, "Well, hello, neighbors. What are you two doing here?" He took one of the four chairs at the table, and sat. "I just came down for lunch. Mind if I join you?"

They were both startled to see him. Tom was first to respond, "Dan! What a surprise. You're the one we came to see. We had no idea where you were. What a coincidence. Are you staying at this hotel, too?"

Mary jumped in, "Oh, Dan! Have you found Mandy? How is she? Where is she?"

"No, Mary, I haven't found her, but I'm getting close."

Just then, a waiter came to take drink orders. When he left, Dan continued.

"Someone took a couple of shots at

me a little while ago, but missed. They really don't want me to find her if they are trying to kill me."

"Shot at, that's awful!" said Mary who was dressed in a black dress with white
flowers. Tom wore a business suit, white
shirt and tie.

"Don't worry about it Mary, I have been shot at many times in my life. I'm fine. I suspect they will make more attempts, but I will be ready next time. Don't worry about me, you two, this is what I was trained to do, and have done it much of my life."

Tom frowned, "How did you get that knot on your head?"

Instinctively, he raised a hand to feel it, "I forgot to duck when I went to my room a few minutes ago." That broke the
seriousness of their conversation, and they
all got a little chuckle out of it.

"Seriously," said Dan, "why have you two come to Frankfurt?"

Tom explained how Mary had insisted because she wanted to be here when Dan found Mandy, she did not want to wait so long to see her.

"Besides," interjected Mary, "I thought there might be something we could do to help."

That made sense to Dan, and he thought perhaps they might be of help. He said, "That just might be a good idea, but just now, let's enjoy our lunch."

The waiter was back with their drinks, and was ready to take their order.

During lunch, Dan told Tom and Mary all the details about his being shot at, and he filled them in with what he had learned and where he was in his investigation.

"We want to help if there is anything we can do," said Tom.

"I will have to think about that, but not right now, there is something I want to try first."

They gave each other their room number, and lingered at lunch to visit. Then, Dan returned to his room. There was a germ of an idea in the back of his head he needed to develop.

CHAPTER 21

The castle-like mansion stood on the top of a small rolling hill, not more than about two-hundred feet high. Dan carefully studied the setting again. From the front door to the street below was a well-kept lawn with green grass that was well manicured. It was a beautiful lawn. A doublewide driveway curved gently upward to pass on the right side of the house and disappear behind the house to the garage at the back. The driveway also divided to provide a drive that circled across to the front of the house, then it continued down the left of the hill down to the street. It had three stories, and he believed Mandy was probably confined on the third floor. It was a beautiful house in a beautiful setting. On the left side of the house, there were a few large trees and shrubs, and on the right side, the mini-forest where he'd approached the first time.

There were no houses across the street, but a heavily wooded area, thick with
trees and underbrush. This was where Dan
secluded himself after parking his new rental car, an Audi, across from the mansion. The binoculars he had purchased were very powerful. He directed them to the front windows. It was almost as if he were standing at the windows, peeping inside, but without lights inside, he could see nothing but shadows moving about in a few windows. He believed he had been shot at, so he figured they were trying to kill him. He was sure the house had some kind of security system that might be difficult to disable, and he was reluctant to just walk right up to the front door as he had done before. After all, they were expecting him, and were prepared to kill him on sight.

Though the strong binoculars he saw things up close and personal. Even if he tried to come at night, they likely had motion sensors that would light him up for a sniper. But he was not without a plan to annoy and confuse them. He smiled.

***

Clara sat alone in the bedroom she and Dietrich shared. She had a problem. Mandy was actually *her* daughter, and she longed to tell her. She wanted desperately to hold her close and tell her she loved her. Her problem was Dietrich. She was sorry she had ever met him, let alone marry him. Her marriage to him had also been a disaster. He was a sorry excuse for a husband. Certainly, she did not love him, and hadn't for a very long time. She wanted to divorce him, and the sooner the better. She thought herself a fool to have ever had anything to do with him. He wanted no children, and he had become a tyrant and abusive verbally

and physically. However, he was Mandy's father, even though he had never intended to be. It was *she* who had tracked down their daughter. She had been forced to give her up for adoption. She was so young, but when he learned she had a daughter who became a child prodigy like he had been; a famous world class, concert pianist, *he* suddenly wanted her. Not because she was his daughter, but because he wanted her to perform with the symphony orchestra he conducted in Frankfurt. His arrogance and pompousness was extreme, his ego blown out of proportion. This obsession for Mandy had driven him out of his mind. She truly believed he was insane. He was a monster at six-feet-four and three-hundred-sixty
pounds. There was no way she could oppose him to his face. What did he think
he was doing when he kidnapped her? He
had never told her what his plans were once he had her.

And then there was Fritz. Just a vassal; Dietrich's cousin, a thug that did his dirty work. He doesn't have the brains God gave a goose, but Dietrich has him guarding Mandy. I can never see her by myself to talk to her. I can't tell her I'm her real mother. The only time I see her is when he makes her practice piano. It was time she and her mom reconciled and had a talk.

She started to get up, but just then, there was a soft knock at the door. She hesitated and sat forward.

"Come in," she said.

It was her mother.

"Clara, honey, we need to have a little talk while Dietrich is at symphony rehearsal. I want us to patch things up. I think we need each other right now"

"I was just about to come looking for you, mom. I wanted to talk to you, too. I had the same thought. It is about time. I'm sorry."

"I'm sorry, too. Then, let's let the past bury the past, ok?

"Sure, mom.

The master bedroom had a nice seating area, and that is where mother and daughter sat.

"What is it you wanted to talk to me about, mother?"

"You first," said Mia.

Clara paused a few moments as she gathered her thoughts. Then she sighed and said, "It's about Mandy."

"That is just what I came to talk to you about. We have to figure out how to free her from Dietrich, she needs to get away and we need to take her back to America where she belongs."

"I know, mother, but I also want to let her know I'm her birth mother. I would like her to be a part of my life now I've found her. I want to rid myself of Dietrich, and want to go back to America with you."

"I understand, honey. That's great, I want that, too."

"I just can't figure out a way to free her with Fritz guarding her all the time."

"We have to find a way to get him out of the equation."

"Yes, but how?"

"I've been thinking about that, and have a suggestion."

"Oh, mother," Clara said excitedly. "Tell me!"

"Suppose I went shopping one day, and instead went to the airport and bought tickets for the three of us back to Washington. Then, we somehow incapacitated both Dietrich and Fritz to give us the time to get on the airplane."

"That sounds like a good plan, but
how could we incapacitate them? Don't you think they would know where we went and follow us?"

"Hm," said Mia. Then her face twisted into a wry smile, "It depends on just how thoroughly incapacitated we make them," and she winked.

Mia went back to her room. She had been thinking about herself lately, thinking she was looking like a frowzy old frump. But she wasn't all that old. Sure, she was pretty big and stout, but she realized she had let herself go for a number of years. She stood before a full length mirror on the back of her bathroom door. She was sixty-seven years old, but still a handsome woman. She had been letting her hair grow longer for the past couple of months. She'd once had lovely hair. It had once been her glory, but somewhere along the way she had let her appearance go to pot, never wearing pretty dresses, cutting her hair in a very masculine way, wearing ugly clunky shoes, and gaining weight. Her excuse was that she would rather be comfortable than attractive. She moved closer to the mirror to look more closely at her face. She studied the contours and shape of her face; blue eyes set neatly apart. Her skin was very young looking, scarcely any wrinkles at all. Her hair had a few streaks of gray, but was mostly a nice, shiny brunette. She wondered

if she should dye it blond, but
thought not. She rubbed her lips
together. Not bad. Some good
makeup, and hair styled, a pretty
dress, nice shoes, and losing a little
weight. She could be quite attractive
again. She would do it. First she
could do something with her hair
right now. It was still somewhat
short, but was long enough she could
make it quite attractive. When
she went to buy plane tickets, she
would
pick up a few nice dresses and shoes.
        In an hour, she was ready to go,
so
She went downstairs to take one of
Dietrich's cars to shop; then to the
airport. It was almost midafternoon.

CHAPTER 22

Dieter Pachman was an ex-
heavyweight boxer. He was six-foot-
six, and built like a fighter; heavy
shoulders and biceps; big chest, and
six-pack abs. He retired from
professional boxing at age 51, and
now worked as a baggage handler at
the airport. He was still in good
shape. He didn't want to fight Dan
Good alone and Fritz had told them
he wanted him dead. Fritz had called
them all together, and Dieter was
glad because he had an idea he
wanted Fritz to consider. The
meeting was in Hermann's
apartment, and when Fritz arrived,
he began yelling at Hermann for
missing his target. Hermann yelled
back. Finally they wound down, and
Fritz glanced around at everyone.

"Alright. Let's get down to business," he said, and they all shifted uneasily in their seats.

"We need stop fooling around, and get this done."

Dieter spoke up, "I have an idea to consider."

Fritz just said, "What?"

"We know the hotel he is in and have his suite number. Why can't we just all of us jump him when he comes out the door of his suite tomorrow morning; the four of us, and club him unconscious, tie him up, and slip him out the back way of the hotel and into a car. Then, we take him out to some secluded area, beat him to death, and leave his body for the animals?"

"I like it, Dieter, but let's think it through a little. There are a lot of details to work out, but that just might work."

The four men began discussing the plan.

***

Unknown to Fritz, Dan was parked
across the street watching the big
house with his powerful binoculars
when Fritz drove down the driveway,
and turned into the street to go meet
with his friends. He quickly started
his Audi rental car and followed.
When Fritz parked at Hermann's
apartment house and went inside,
Dan got out and went to Fritz's car
and deftly slashed all four of his tires.
Before he left, Dan put a slip of paper
under one of his windshield wipers.
Then, he drove away.

***

Upon his return to his car, Fritz was
so preoccupied with the new plan to
eliminate Dan Good, he did not notice
his tires had been slashed. He didn't
even notice the paper under a
windshield wiper until he tried to pull
it out into the street. When his eye
caught the paper, he stopped where
he was; half out of his parallel slot.

He opened his car door, jumped out to grab the paper and read, "Tired?" He frowned. That made no sense to him, so he got in the car, started to pull away from the curb. He immediately realized he had a flat tire. He got out to look, and found all four tires had been slashed. He went berserk, yelling German curse words at the top of his lungs. He kicked the tires, threw his arms in the air and shook his fists in the air. Now the note made sense, and he knew this must be the work of Dan Good. He'd been followed. That meant Dan Good knew where they were keeping that girl, and that he must have been watching the house when he drove away. He had to tell Dietrich as soon as possible, but it would take a lot of time to get the car fitted with new tires. He was beside himself with anger. When he calmed down a little, he looked around the street. He wondered if Good was still around, watching, but he saw no sign of him.

When he finally arranged to get new tires put on the car, he found a pay phone inside the apartment building and called to tell Dietrich what had happened to make him late returning.

Dietrich was outraged, and cursed loudly, disturbing the household staff. Mia and Clara were greatly amused by the whole thing, and were happy he was so angry. Even though they'd heard only one side of the phone conversation, Dietrich had clearly revealed the gist of the situation. They needed to find a way they might contact Dan.

Dietrich and Fritz agreed that the
house was likely well protected by alarms in and outside the house. They believed Dan Good would not be able to get into the house without their knowledge, but little did they know about Dan's tricks.

***

By the time Fritz called Dietrich, Dan was back across the street from the big house, watching with the powerful binoculars. Clouds had come to darken the sky, and the air was getting quite cool. The Audi was parked in plain sight across the street, and Dan was sitting inside; a crossbow was on the seat beside him with a quiver of arrows on the floor. In the gathering darkness, Dan slipped out of the car and sneaked into the wooded area behind him till he was sure he could not be seen from the house. He had the crossbow and quiver of arrows, and wore night-vision goggles. He placed an arrow in the crossbow, and let it fly up the hill. The arrow slammed into the front door with a loud thump. He quickly sent three more. He wasn't sure anyone in the house could hear them, but the sound of them seemed quite loud to him. He had no idea when they might discover the arrows, but as he started to go back to the car, he heard the big front doors open, and Dietrich, himself, came out of the house to find the arrows.

That should give him pause.

***

Four arrows were stuck into his front door! Dietrich was both astounded and confused. What a strange thing! It could only be the work of Dan Good, he reasoned as he squinted into the early evening darkness. He could make out a dark car parked across the street, but could see no one. If it was Dan Good, why would he shoot arrows into his doors? It was insane to him. What did Good think he was doing? How could he think it could help him to get to Mandy? It was a silly and useless thing to do. It must mean something to him, but what?

Then he thought of Fritz's tires being slashed. It's just harassment, he thought. The man was just trying harassing him. Well, it was working. He felt harassed.

Suddenly another arrow zoomed into the door. It missed hitting him by less than a foot. He jumped at the sound. Then, he saw there was a note wrapped around the arrow. He removed it and read it. "I'm coming for her," was all it said. Not only was Dietrich confused about the incident, he was quite frightened. This was bizarre.

CHAPTER 23

Monday, September 15, 1986

An old, dilapidated Volkswagen bus came to a stop in the alley near the service entrance of the Steigenberger hotel at 7 a.m. Four big burly men got out. Each had a wooden club about two feet long attached to his belt. A sister of one of the men worked as a maid in the hotel. It was she who opened the locked service entrance door for them to come inside. Dan Good's suite was on the top floor. The man's sister disappeared, and the three men took the back stairs, moving up quietly.

The biggest flaw in Dieter's plan was that they had no idea what time of the morning Dan Good would emerge from his rooms. It seems no one had thought of that.

When they got up to his floor, they stopped on the top step to survey the hallway before continuing. Then they stepped on to the landing and walked down the hall looking at the numbers on the doors. Dan's suite was near the elevators. Upon reaching his door, they suddenly didn't know what to do. No one had a clue when Dan would come out, so they just milled about until they figured out that they needed to position themselves on either side of the door to be able to attack him immediately as he came out. They stood awkwardly waiting and foolishly wondering if and when he might appear.

Dan was about to leave his suite when his sharp ears heard the soft shuffling just outside his door. He peeped out the peephole, and saw four big men shuffling around. Each had a club attached at their waist. Two things happened at the same time. First, an elevator door opened, and a cleaning lady came onto the floor pushing a large cart with cleaning equipment, clean sheets, towels and washrags. As one might expect, the cart had a wheel that squeaked loudly. Then, no sooner than she appeared, the doorknob turned, and Dan suddenly came out. The men were turned to look at the maid coming toward them. That brief distraction enabled Dan to slam a big fist into one man full in his face on his nose. He dropped the club he was holding, and blood gushed as he fell backward to sit on the floor bleeding badly. Dan then swung an elbow on the jaw of a second man, and he heard the jawbone crack. He, too, dropped his club and fell to the floor. The third man tried to hit Dan on the head with his club, but Dan grabbed the end of the club, jerked it out of his hand throwing the man off balance, and then he poked that man in his eye with the other end of the club. It was hard enough to crack his jaw and black his eye. Dan's movements were as a blinding flash, so he even managed to bury a fist hard into the fourth man's solar plexus. It knocked the wind out of him, and he crumpled to the floor in a heap, gasping for breath.

The poor chambermaid clasped both her hands to her mouth, yet managed to render an earth-shattering scream. She turned and ran back into the elevator, leaving her cart as she pressed the down button, and continued screaming. Dan pulled out his Glock.

He had them all get back up and sit on the floor in the hallway, and stood over them waving his gun from one to the other. Blood was everywhere, staining the fine carpet. He grabbed a hand full of towels off the cleaning cart, and tossed them to each man. They put them over the areas that were bleeding. There was no fight left in any of them.

"I assume you thugs were sent by Dietrich to try to murder me. Well, you can go back and tell him you failed again. Tell him I'm coming after him. I am going to get him, and I'm going to take Mandy home where she belongs. He can't stop me. Now, get out of here before I shoot you."

It took only moments for them to be up and able to leave; scrambling away as fast as they could.

After they were gone, the maid's report to the hotel management brought the manager and the German police up to his suite. When they finally came, it was fortunate that Dan spoke German, and was able to convince them that he had no idea who tried to attacked him or why. He explained that they all just ran away down the back stairs. He had also hidden his gun back in his room, so when they searched him, he was clean. Management would have the carpet cleaned soon, and the police said they were going to try to find the men who'd attacked him. Finally, Dan was free to go. He grabbed a couple of things he would need when he called on Sondheim again. Then he called Tom and Mary. He would meet them at Oscar's to have breakfast, only now it would be nearer brunch.

***

A broken nose, broken jawbone, and a broken eye socket needed tending to before they could do anything else, and the blow Dan gave the one in the solar plexus rendered that man in serious pain and trauma. They had a difficult time deciding whether they should go to the hospital for treatment, but finally decided they would each just go home to let their wife do what she could. Driving the bus was also a problem, but eventually, the man with the solar plexus injury was best able to drive. They left as quickly as they could, hoping they could get away before the police found them in the alley, and they did.

When Fritz got home, he had the privilege to tell Dietrich what had happened. Dietrich had just finished having brunch. He'd slept late. Fritz reluctantly told him he would like to speak to him in the library. It was there Dietrich exploded in anger, and cursed him to his face. He told him to get out of his house and go home. He didn't want ever to see his face again. He didn't want his help anymore; he would deal with Dan Good himself.

After Fritz had gone to his room to pack his things, Dietrich went to find Clara. She and Mia were just coming out of their bedroom, and were startled to see Dietrich coming toward them.

"Clara," he said, "we need to talk. Come with me." He hardly looked at Mia as he took Clara's hand and escorted her down to the library. They sat in facing chairs.

"I have decided we need to move Mandy to another location. I have kicked Fritz out. He is useless. I don't want Dan Good to find us. We will move to my father's house in Westend. It is empty, you know, but I still own it and maintain it. The old family upright piano is still there, and

I am going to have it tuned for Mandy to use to practice."

This gave Clara the opening she wanted, "You have never told me *why* you want Mandy here in Germany, and insist she keep practicing her piano? What are you planning?"

He looked at her strangely, and thought for a long time before he answered.

"She is my *daughter*," he said, as
though she didn't know this. "She is a world class pianist," he reasoned. What he said next was shocking.

"Of course I want to show her off *here* in Frankfurt, my home town. Here in my country," he added. "I want her to do a concert with me as a guest artist. I want to conduct the orchestra. I am planning for her to play Tchaikovsky's No. 1, what else? I have it all worked out."

Clara's jaw dropped. "You can't be so stupid. Have you gone crazy? You're insane! You have lost your mind."

"What are you talking about? She is your daughter, too. You should be thrilled."

Clara shouted, "Yes! Mandy is well known all over the world! You kidnapped her, and Dan Good is here to find her and take her home to her adoptive parents. The FBI in America is looking for her as well. They will arrest you as soon as she surfaces. They will arrest you and put you in prison for kidnapping."

"What are you talking about? You don't understand," he stammered. "She was never harmed. We treated her grandly, took good care of her. She is fine. They will congratulate me after the great performance."

Clara stood. He didn't look right in his eyes. Surely, he had lost his mind. He was beyond reason.

"You're a fool," she shouted at him. I am leaving you. I am going to take Mandy back to America, and I'm going to divorce you. I want nothing more to do with you."

"I won't have you talk to me like that. I'm going to beat you black and blue."

Dietrich started to get up from his chair, but suddenly there was a loud clang,
as a big, black, heavy iron skillet hit him hard on the back of his head. Mia had taken the skillet from the kitchen, and slipped into the library silently as the two were arguing. She had swung the big skillet as hard as she possibly could, hoping to kill him. Dietrich dropped to the floor and sprawled out to lie still.

"I hope you killed him, mother."

"I intended to." Mia took a close look. "No, he is still breathing. We must tie him up securely. Do you know where there is some rope we can use?"

Clara looked around the room, "No,
but the windows have heavy cords on the drapes that we can use. They look plenty strong enough. Help me get them."

The two women worked quickly and efficiently in gathering the cords and tying Dietrich securely. Mia went through his pockets until she found his keys. When they were satisfied he was not going anywhere, they went back upstairs to the third floor to free Mandy. Mia stuck the key into the lock.

Mandy heard the key in the door, and believed it was either Fritz or fat man. She quickly picked up the vanity stool and hid behind the door. She would smash the stool over the head of which ever had come for her. She held it tight like a baseball bat intending to swing it hard into the face of the intruder.

CHAPTER 24

Fritz was angry. He and Dietrich were first cousins, and had grown up together. They had been close all their lives, but now, he was kicking him out of his house. He packed his things and went to the garage for his car. As he drove away from the estate, he decided not to go back to his apartment. Instead, he would go try to find Dan Good and kill him, himself. He and his friends had bungled the job, but he would not. He believed he knew exactly where Dan Good was staying. Dan Good would not know him when he saw him, he thought. He also had the perfect weapon, a very sharp six-inch hunting knife.

He drove straight to the Steigenberger, but did not park near the hotel. It was a while before lunch, but the streets were crowded with people rushing about. He hardly noticed the people; he was so intently focused on getting to Dan Good's suite as fast as he could. He walked into the front entrance, and took the elevator to the top floor. He walked to the door of Dan's suite, and knocked loudly. Nothing. He waited, and waited. Perhaps he must not in. Not knowing where he might be, he wasn't sure what to do. Then he remembered that Oscar's was just next door. He would go down to the restaurant, have a beer and think about where he might be. Or, he thought, maybe he would just wait and watch for him to come back to the hotel. He had a good view of the entrance.

As he entered the restaurant, he was surprised to see Dan Good sitting at a table with a man and a woman. They evidently had just finished eating, and were getting up to leave. This was his opportunity. He could just walk past the big man and swiftly drive the knife into his heart and walk away. He won't know what hit him. By the time people realize what happened, he will be long gone.

***

The door opened, and Mandy swung the stool with all her might, but her aim was high, thinking it would be fat man or Fritz who were both very tall. Of course, Mia was tall for a woman, so the stool hit a glancing blow high on her head. So even though she was hit hard, the stool continued quickly upward and hit the side of the doorway on her follow through. The stool broke in pieces in her hands.

Mia was stunned, and fell to the floor, moaning. The blow did cut her head a little. She bled quite a bit as heads do, but it was not fatal. Immediately, Mandy realized who she had hit, and dropped down beside her. Clara also rush to her mother's side.

Mandy cried, "Oh, I am so sorry. I

thought it was the men coming for me."

"Mother," cried Clara. She looked at Mandy, "You killed her!"

Mia suddenly moaned loudly, and began a feeble flailing.

"She's alive," said Mandy. "I'll get a wet rag, she's bleeding." She ran to her bathroom to wet a washrag.

When Mandy returned, Clara had rolled Mia over onto her back so they could tend to her injury better.

"I am so sorry," said Mandy, again.

"She is going to have a big goose egg, but the cut isn't too bad. I'm going to get something to bandage her head." Clara fled.

When she came back, the two of them helped Mia to a chair. Mandy got her a drink of water from her bathroom; there was an extra clean glass. Mandy then went to get a clean, cool washrag to lay on her head.

Soon Mia was alert and coherent.

"Mandy," said Clara, "help me get her up. We have a lot to tell you, but we need to get moving first."
As the three made their way down to the garage to get a car, Clara said, "We are taking you back to America. We have tied Dietrich up in the library, and he kicked Fritz out of the house, so it is just we girls now. Let's get you packed. Mom and I are already packed."

In Mandy's room, they quickly had her packed, and headed down to the garage. it was then Clara noticed her mother's new appearance.

"Mother! You look absolutely gorgeous! When did you morph into such a lovely butterfly?"

"That is a very pretty dress," added Mandy.

Mia's dress was a navy blue with a fancy array of pearls festooned over the bodice.

"I still have a few tricks up my sleeve," said Mia with a nice smile.

At the garage, they chose
Dietrich's big Mercedes, and speed
away toward the airport.

***

An hour later, in the library, Dietrich
was waking up. He looked around to
try to orient himself, but he could
barely move. He was tied up. Why?
His head really hurt. What
happened? He had no memory of the
skillet bashing into the back of his
head. Everything had just gone
black. It had happened so fast, but
he did remember talking with Clara
before. Clara? Where was she? He
was still in the library, but alone and
bound and he was lying on the floor.
What time was it? Where were the
servants?

　The one thing Mia and Clara
had not thought to do was to gag
him. He began shouting for help at
the top of his lungs.

　Klaus, the butler, was just
coming down the hall, and heard his

master calling loudly. He hurried toward the sound. It was coming from the library.

When he opened the door, he was astonished to see his master trussed up on the floor. He rushed to help him.

"Klaus," he yelled. "Where have you been? It seems like I have been yelling for an hour."

"I'm sorry, sir. I was at the back of the house with the other servants. How did you get tied up?"

"Never mind that, just untie me and help me up. We must try to find Clara and her mother. Quickly!"

"Oh. I'm sorry, sir, I just saw them
drive away. I thought there was someone else with them."

"No!" Dietrich screamed. He knew they had freed Mandy. Where were they taking her? He tried to think, but his head hurt so badly it made thinking difficult. Then, he thought, *They are going to take Mandy back to the States. They are going to the airport. I must stop them..*

Dietrich said to his butler, "Come help me pack. I have to go to America as soon as I can." Then an afterthought, "And call Fritz. Tell him to come meet me at the airport as fast as he can, I want him to go with me."

***

Dan was getting up from the table when, out of the corner of his eye, in his peripheral vision, he noticed a man suddenly change the direction he was walking, and was headed his way. He avoided looking directly at him, but watched him in his peripheral vision. He saw the man would pass so near him he would almost rub shoulders. Then the man's right hand swiftly swung toward him. He had a knife and was about to plunge it into his heart, but Dan was faster. His left hand came up to block the man's arm, pushing it upward. His movement was so quick and powerful, it knocked the knife out of his hand, then he grabbed the man's wrist with his left hand and twisted his arm around behind him. Then his right arm closed around the man's neck. He had the man in a chokehold. The man was big and powerfully built, but was no match for Dan's power and skill. There was nothing the man could do, but struggle.

"Tom," said Dan casually, "Call the police."

CHAPTER 25

Mandy had learned the names of the two women, and their relationship to each other while they had helped her pack, but it was as they were driving to the Frankfurt airport that she learned that Clara was her birthmother and Mia her grandmother. Tom and Mary Lynn were the only parents she had ever known, though they had told her when she was twelve that she was adopted at birth. She had never been interested or concerned as to who her birthmother was, but now she was overwhelmed by this revelation; thrilled and excited. They told her about themselves and their lives until Clara found her just before Dietrich kidnapped her, and they told her why she was kidnapped. The three of them bonded very quickly, and they were all full of joy. Her mother and grandmother wanted to be a part of her life, and she wanted them as well. The car was filled with laughter and teers. The only negative thing she learned was that Dietrich Sondheim was her biological father. Of course she was very angry with him, and she wanted absolutely nothing to do with him. Her mother and grandmother believed he was insane. She was thrilled they were taking her home now. She was anxious to introduce them to her adoptive parents.

***

By the time Dietrich reached the airport in
Frankfurt, he saw no sign of the three women, and a flight to the United States had already left. He assumed they were on that flight, so he booked the next flight. It would be over two hours later, but he bought two seats; one for him and one for Fritz.

   After a while, HE began to

wonder why Fritz had not come yet. He was getting nervous, and went searching for a pay phone. He called his house, and his butler, Klaus, answered.

"Where is Fritz," Dietrich demanded, "he isn't here yet?" He was almost shouting into the phone.

Klaus quickly moved the phone away from his ear, and said, "I regret to tell you, sir, but I have not been able to reach him. He isn't answering his home phone." Perhaps he has not arrived there yet."

"He doesn't live that far away. I'm sure he's in his apartment by now."

"Then he must have gone somewhere else," offered Klaus.

Dietrich yelled a string of curse words
into the phone and hung up.

Where could that idiot have gone?

Again, he cursed under his breath as he went to cancel the second seat.

Later, as the time drew near for his flight, Dietrich heard his name paged, he had a phone call. When he answered, it was Klaus again.

"I just got a call from Fritz's lawyer, sir," he said. "He told me Fritz wanted to tell you he has been arrested for attempted murder, and could you come to post his bail."

"Murder? Who did he try to murder?" Then he thought, and said, "No. He's a fool and a bumbler. I don't want my name to be associated with his anymore." He cursed again, and hung up. He would go to America alone.

***

After Fritz was arrested, Tom and Mary returned to their suite. Once inside, where no one could hear them, Tom immediately exclaimed, "I have never seen anything like that in my life; what Dan did!"

"It was over before I even noticed anything it was so fast. I didn't see any of it," said Mary.

"That man is amazing, Mary."

"They made Dan go with them to the police station. I hope he is alright."

"He'll be fine, I'm sure," said Tom. "But in the meantime, why don't you and I go out to Dietrich's house. Dan told us he was the conductor of the Frankfurt Symphony Orchestra. His address will be easy enough to find."

Mary clapped, "Oh, Tom, what a great idea! We can tell him we are Mandy's adoptive parents. Surely he can't refuse to see us."

It was indeed a simple matter, so it wasn't long till they arrived by taxi in front of the mansion.

Tom knocked boldly on the door. It was opened by Klaus.

Tom said, "We are Mr. and Mrs. Lynn
from America, and we are here to see Maestro Stroheim, please."

Klaus frowned and shrugged. He shook his head and spread his hands. He did not speak English.

Tom turned to Mary, "What are we to do? I had no idea he would not speak English."

Just then, Klaus touched Tom's arm to get his attention, then held up an index finger, turned and shouted in German.

In moments, a breathless young woman appeared. She was obviously a maid. They conversed a few minutes in German, then the young lady stepped forward to speak to Tom and Mary.

"I'm Mrs. Stroheim's personal maid.
I speak a little English. How may we help you?"

Tom spoke again, "We are Tom and Mary Lynn from America, and we have come to see our daughter. Mandy. We believe he has her in custody."

"She was here, but we just learned my lady and her mother are taking her back to America. I believe that Mr. Sondheim has gone to follow them."

"Oh," said Mary, "Tom, we must go home immediate!"

They turned and ran back to their waiting taxi. They would pack and go to the airport as fast as they could. When they were in the taxi and going back to their hotel, Mary said, "Tom, we need to tell Dan what has happened, but we don't know where is, what can we do?"

"We'll leave a message for him at the hotel desk."

"Great idea, hon."

***

It was late afternoon when Dan managed to get back to his hotel, he wanted to talk to Tom and Mary. As he entered, the desk man called his name, "Mr. Good!"

He went to the desk, and the clerk handed him the message. It read, "Mandy has been freed and is flying home. We are flying home now.

Just wanted you to know. Thanks, Tom and Mary."

Freed? How, and by whom? Why am I the last to know?"

***

Dietrich Schneider, now inflight, pondered his plight. His anger and frustration were out of control, he wanted to kill them all, but although he was very big, he was not athletic at all, nor was he skilled in fighting or weaponry. He still wanted Mandy back with him to play a concert with him conducting the Frankfurt Symphony Orchestra. He did not understand how delusional that idea was. He really had no plan, yet. He had time to think, so he rubbed his eyes and tilted his seat back to think, but he went to sleep instead.

CHAPTER 26

Tuesday, September 16, 1986

When Mandy, Clara and Mia landed at Dulles International, they boarded a taxi, and gave him the address. It was early morning, still dark when they drove onto the Lynn estate in McLean. The three women got out of the taxi, gathered their baggage, and stood at the door of a very dark house as the taxi drove away.

Mandy rang the doorbell, and then knocked loudly on the front door and yelled, "Mom, Dad! It's me Mandy! I'm home!"

It was some minutes before a sleepy eye peeked out the little hole to see Mandy and two other women. Then the door swung open to reveal Bess, the housekeeper, in her robe and slippers.

"Mandy? How nice to see you again. Your parents called last night to tell us you were coming back. They went to Germany to find you, so they are on their way home, now. Come in. Who are your friends?"

Mandy hugged Bess, and introduced Clara as her birthmother, and Mia as her grandmother. Bess was surprised, but readily welcomed them. Then two other servants appeared.

"Let's get a couple of bedrooms ready, and you back into your old room. I guess you all need some sleep, since it will be another hour or so till sunup."

"Thanks, Bess," said Mandy, "but we slept some on the plane. You all go on back to bed. We'll get ourselves settled into our rooms, and wait for mom and dad.

The staff left, and after Mandy, Clara, and Mia were settled in their respective bedrooms, Mandy made breakfast, and the three sat in the breakfast nook.

"I have to warn you, Mandy," said Clara, "I don't know what Dietrich might do when he finds out what mom and I have done. He will be very angry. He seems to have gone mad. He is irrational and unreasonable. I am afraid of him."

"Well," said Mandy. "if he comes over here, he will have our next door neighbor, Dan Good, to deal with. Dan will take good care of all of us. I've decided to move back into my parent's house for a while."

"That's a good idea," said Mia. "Clara and I may have some problems with Dietrich since she is moving back with me in Woodbridge. Frankly we are both afraid he will come after us."

"I'll see if Dan will provide some assistance for you, after all, you are family
now," said Mandy.

"Thank you," said Clara.

The phone suddenly rang, and Mandy grabbed it quickly, "Hello?"

"Mandy? It's Dan. I'm at the Frankfort airport about to board.

Just think you should know; Dietrich is ahead of me by a couple of hours, and he on his way to DC. It might be good if all of you go over to my place until I can get there. I called Kathleen, and she is awake and said to tell you she would be looking for you. Have your parents arrived yet?"

"Hi, Dan. Thanks for the heads up. Mom and dad are not here yet. We will take your advice, and scoot on over to your place as soon as they get here."

"Take your household staff with you, we don't want them at risk," Dan added.

"I will. Thanks again."

Mandy didn't know when she might expect Tom and Mary, but it wasn't but a few minutes until she heard them come into the house.. They were overwhelmed that Mandy was home, and safe. They were quite pleased to meet Clara, Mandy's birthmother, and Mia, Mandy's grandmother. It took them all almost an hour to get everyone settled and over to Dan and Kathleen's place.

Kathleen was delighted to help, of course. It would be their hideout when Dietrich arrived.

"We don't know just how soon Dietrich will get here," said Clara.

"I called Dulles," Kathleen responded. "There is a flight due in within the hour, he might be on it. Then Dan should be here soon after. You will all be quite safe here, and I am happy to be of help."

Mia spoke up, "I've been thinking. Perhaps Clara and I should call a cab and go to my place. I'm not afraid of that big fat oaf."

"I am," said Clara.

"I know, darling, but I have my own big, heavy, iron skillet, and I have my girls at the house."

"I don't think that is a good idea, Mia," said Kathleen. "Please wait here with us until Dan returns. Dietrich might not hurt your girls, but I don't think worth the risk for you two to go. Dan will be here soon enough."

Kathleen had been going over several possible scenarios in her mind of just what Dietrich might do after arriving in America, and she'd decided someone should be staking out Tom and Mary's house. He would surely go there first. Of course, there was no one as capable of doing that than she, so she excused herself, and went to collect a couple of things she thought she might need, and walked next door.

***

Upon landing, Dietrich had worked out a few things in his head. He'd used his true name when he booked this time. He had been thinking things through for hours, and felt he had everything he wanted to do sorted out in his twisted mind. Basically, he wanted to kill everybody.

His mother-in-law was at the top of his list. It was she that had allowed Mandy to almost escape. She was the one who had continued to poison Clara's mind against him; ever since she'd married him. And he had determined that it had to have been Mia who had hit him from behind while he was trying to talk to Clara. Then it was Mia that had talked Clara into freeing Mandy and taking her back to America. She was the one behind all his troubles. She would be the first to die.

Clara would be next. She would be likely be with her mother. It just made sense that she would be the next to die. The two of them were probably Mia's home.

Then he would kill Mandy's adoptive parents. Mandy would no longer have a reason not to stay with him. He was her true father, and together they will become the sensation of the music world; father and daughter traveling and performing together.

Dan Good was just an interfering nuisance He would kill him as well.

He went to the Car Rental counter, and rented a black Chevrolet sedan. Timing was of the essence. He drove straight to Mia's home in Woodbridge. He knew it was risky so early in the day. The sun was just coming up. He had the skill he would need to kill, but he wasn't able to bring his gun on the plane. He had to find some kind of a weapon. The very air was electric. He could feel it. In his mind he wanted to squeeze the life out of them with his bare hands, but knew that wasn't a good option.

It was a very long drive from Dulles out to Woodbridge, Virginia, a DC suburb, and it was quiet as a graveyard as he approached her house. The lights were on in the house. That meant they were all up. He parked down the street at a good long distance away, the sky was clear, and the streetlight was dark as the sun was coming up. No cars were to be seen anywhere; there wasn't another house nearby. It didn't look as though Mia was there. He saw no sign of her car, but it could be in the garage, of course. The garage door was closed. He sat and watched the house for a while. He turned to look up and down the road again, then slipped noiselessly from the car. He walked as silently as he could around the side of the house to see if Mia's car was in the garage. He peered through a small window in the garage door. It wasn't there. He saw a door in the side of the garage. It was not locked, so he slipped inside. He looked around and spotted a tire iron leaning against a wall. That would be his weapon, he thought. He went to get it. It felt good in his hands. Then he looked up and saw an ax hanging on the wall. Much better, he thought, so he traded weapons. He leaned the tire iron against the wall. It was an extraordinary feeling to contemplate killing them all with an ax. He assumed Mia and Clara were inside the house with all Mia's household staff. He swore through clinched teeth. It would not be so easy after all with so many people, he went back to his car to think.

Dietrich began to think about the size of Mia's house. Her husband had been a successful banker in Frankfurt, and had left her a wealthy widow. He resented his mother-in-law's wealth. She had done nothing to get her wealth, but he'd worked hard for his, and he was not nearly as wealthy as she. It wasn't easy for musicians.

He suddenly got out of the car, and started to walk back to the front door. He wanted to wait inside so as to surprise them when they came home. Then he stopped. No! Mia's maids were there. Instead, he went back to his car again. He would wait a while to see if Mia showed up, and in minutes his head rolled back on the headrest.

Half an hour later, he awoke with a jerk, surprised he'd gone to sleep. Why had Mia and Clara not returned, he wondered. Where could they have gone? He was wasting his time, he decided. He couldn't just sit here all day, so he drove away in disgust.

CHAPTER 27

There was a blue sky, and no rain in DC when Dan came out of the plane to ride in the tram to the terminal; even the wind was calm. He picked up his bag at the baggage claim, and went out to take a cab home. It was going to be a beautiful day. He felt compelled to go home first to see Kathleen. He missed her terribly, and she was most important to him.

On the way, he reviewed the situation. He knew Dietrich didn't know his address, but he knew the address of the Lynn's. Dietrich most likely would go directly to Mia's home. He would find only her staff there, so he might head then head over to the Lynn's home. That meant that everybody was safe and sound under the watchful eye of Kathleen. She was indeed a true treasure to him. He did not know how violent Dietrich might be. He believed nobody was currently in any danger.

The cab rolled up to his front door, and Kathleen came bounding out to greet him. They went back inside as the cab drove away. Dan was glad to see everyone safe and sound, and to visit a few minutes..

He'd slept on the plane, but needed to take a shower and change clothes. Soon he was back downstairs.

"I am going to run over to your place, Mia. I want to be sure it is safe for you and Clara before you go there," said Dan. "I'll try not to be long. Kathleen gave me your address."

"Check on my girls while you are there, please, Dan," said Mia.

"I'll do that."

Brenda had gone back to Dallas, so Dan, a bit amused thinking of her love to drive his Mustang, took the Mustang. The convertible top was up, so he switched on WGMS to listen to the classical music on his way. It was playing Hayden's 89th symphony. He loved Hayden.

Kathleen decided she would go outside to find a spot she could watch Tom and Mary's house in case Dietrich showed up there. She got some good binoculars, and a comfortable folding chair, and some small pillows.

***

Where was Dietrich, wondered Ludwig von Stoddard, the first violinist of the Frankfurt Symphony Orchestra? The orchestra had assembled for rehearsal, but their conductor was late. Too late, thought von Stoddard; it was getting on to be an hour.

Ludmilla Neumann, Dietrich's associate conductor, went to call his home. Upon returning, she expressed her great dismay by announcing, "That man has lost his mind. I just talked to his butler, and he told me Maestro Dietrich has flown to America again without telling us. I don't understand what has got into him lately. He has been not showing up for rehearsals and changing our schedules and even the programs that have already been scheduled. I'm going to the Symphony Association. Something needs to be done about him immediately. The man's gone mad. You all may go home. We'll call you when I find out what the Association wants to do." She dismissed the musicians.

***

Dan turned off I-95 at the exit for Woodbridge, and wound his way around to the road where Mia's house stood. He slowed to about 10 miles an hour so he could survey the area he was entering. He stopped. He saw no cars on the road. Dietrich wasn't here. He pulled over to the side of the road. He thought Dietrich might have hidden his car, but saw no sign of it. He saw the maids were up, so he checked out the surrounding area outside the house just in case. He found nothing. Dietrich must have been here at some point and left.

He went to check on Mia's maids, and told them where she and Clara were. He reassured them their mistress would be returning soon, and feeling they would be alright, went back to his car, and drove Away.

CHAPTER 28

He had bought a map, so he pulled over on the side of a road in Woodbridge to study it. He knew the address. It took him a while, but he found the fastest way to the Lynn home in McLean. He plotted the route, and highlighted it with a yellow marker. It was on the northwest side of DC. The drive would be long in the Washington traffic no matter how he went. He somehow had to kidnap Mandy again. He would kill the Lynn's if necessary. If Mia and Clara were there, he'd kill them, too. He did not know Dan Good had a home next door.

Suddenly, there was a loud rapping sound on his window. It scared the life out of him. He looked up into the face of a Highway Patrolman in full uniform, and

wearing sunglasses. It threw him into a sudden fit of rage. He opened his car door so quickly, it knocked the officer off balance, and Dietrich grabbed the ax as he jumped out of the car, and swung it at the officer. It hit him a devastating blow between his shoulder and head, cutting him deeply into his body. It shattered his collarbone as it plunged into the man. A
second swing hit him in the side of his
head, splitting his head open and killing him instantly.

Dietrick was surprised by what he'd just done. Spattered in blood, he sat back in his car and drove quickly away. He'd killed a patrolman. Now what was he going to do? He had to find some place to change clothes, and get cleaned up. He was glad he had his suitcases.

Dietrich began to wonder how long it would be before that officer might be found. After thinking about it, he believed he had left

nothing to identify himself as the
killer, and smiled.

He wondered why Clara and Mia
had never arrived at Mia's house.
That is where they should have been.
The thought raised his anger.

*Ach! They took Mandy to her
adoptive parent's house.*

He merged into I-95 North, and
soon found himself making his way
through the great city of Washington,
DC. He didn't realize the traffic
would be so heavy. He should have
gone around the beltway, but now it
was too late. Many, he figured, were
tourists on their way to the many
great monuments, museums, and
other sites that were abundant in the
Nation's Capital. He'd already
forgotten about the officer he'd
killed and never considered the furor
it
would cause in law enforcement to
find his
murderer.

When he entered Georgetown
Pike, he drove slowly, straining to see
the addresses. A couple of cars

honked at him, then sped around his when they were able, but he paid them no attention.

Wait! I must have passed it.

He found a place to turn around, and drove even slower.

***

Kathleen was comfortably seated in a small folding chair which she had cushioned with the small pillows. She was about thirty yards from the Lynn's property. If Dietrich came, he would never see her, but she could watch him closely with the small but powerful binoculars hanging around her neck.

The blaring horns alerted her.

"Blow your nose, you'll get more out of it," she thought.

People did honk sometimes, but seldom so persistent. She raised her glasses to see a car drive slowly by the house, but it didn't tune into the drive. Then, in just a few moments, she heard another long, loud blast of horn, and the car she'd seen before returned very slowly, and this time it turned into Tom's and Mary's drive. She watched as it came up to the house and stopped. When he slowly creeped out of the car, she was startled to see him carrying an ax.

What was he planning to do with that,
hack them to death? This man is very crazy and dangerous.

She was not about to confront him with that horrid thing. She would just see
what he did.

Dietrich, with hunched shoulders, began to encircle the big house, peeking in windows along his way. He went all the
way around the house, also trying to find
an open door or window.

Kathleen continued to watch him till he disappeared around the back of the place. Then in a few moments, he reappeared at the front. She could see the tension in his body. He obviously thought that Clara and Mia had brought Mandy here. That's why he came. He suddenly raised the ax up high, shaking it, and cursed a blue streak out loud in German epithets.

That ought to turn the air blue.

Then he threw the ax as hard as he could into a front window near the door. The glass shattered. He rushed forward to use his elbows to make a larger opening, and crawled inside through the broken window.

What is he up to now?

She could hear him smashing things, probably with that ax, she thought. He must be venting his anger by destroying Tom and Mary's furniture. Kathleen laid down her binoculars, and hurried back inside.

She shouted, "Tom! Call the cops. He's destroying your house with an ax.

It would solve a lot of problems if he could get arrested, thought Kathleen, but he'd be gone before they could get here.

Dietrich thrashed about a bit, then came out the front door, not bothering to shut it, and he, with his ax, got in the car, and drove away. Kathleen came out just in time to see him leave, and wondered where he was going now. She rushed over to their house to see what damage he'd done. The Lynn's and their staff followed her. At least they were all alright, thought Kathleen, but poor Mary and Tom and Mandy; their house.

Several chairs and small tables were destroyed, and there were a few holes in the walls. But, he'd also taken his ax to the big grand piano. Mandy will be devastated; she had grown up with that piano. The servants told Kathleen there was no damage upstairs, it was all done in that downstairs livingroom area. Dietrich was gone, so It was time they went back to her house.

She went out the front door, and heard the familiar sound of Dan's Mustang coming up the driveway.

When he stopped and got out of the
car, she flung herself into his arms.

"What are you doing over here?"

"I decided Tom's and Mary's house needed to be staked out, and it's a good thing I did." Then, she told him all Dietrich had done to their neighbor's house.

"I have no idea, of course, where he went when he left."

"Never mind, sweetheart," said Dan, "let's go home."

CHAPTER 29

Thirteen year old Johnny Thorn was biking his way home from a friend's house when he noticed that a Highway Patrolman's car was on the side of the road in front of him, and the driver's side door was ajar. As he came closer, he saw the officer lying crumpled in a kind of bloody heap. That really scared him, so he quickly peddled home, and told his mother, who then called it in.

Other Highway Patrol officers were soon on the scene with paramedics. Before touching anything, of course, they cordoned off the crime scene. The officer was dead, so they called for forensics and the ME.

Since Woodbridge was the closest town to the scene, and they had only two detectives, Dianna

Smart and James Stoddard on their meager staff, they arrived just as the ME and forensics' team were finishing up. The photographer was still taking pictures. Smart and Stoddard had been partners for nearly five years now. She was the lead, and was ten years older than he. They stood silently, contemplating the crime scene. The wind had come up, and was rustling the trees. The area was a place of extraordinary beauty, and about a half mile from the nearest house. Now the area was marred by a ghastly murder.

"The officer's name was Brandon McFarlane. He had a wife and three small daughters," said Smart.

"Yeah," said Stoddard, "now she's a twenty-seven year old widow with three little girls left stranded."

Frank Ferguson, the ME, stood and looked at the two Detectives. He pulled off his gloves. "Looks like you guys got an ax murderer to look for.

Somebody hacked this poor man to death."

"Yuk," said Dianna.

"Yeah. Just two strikes; one between his shoulder and head," he went on. "Don't know for sure if it was an ax or hatchet, but I think ax because it cut so deep into him. Then the other strike was on the left side of his head, splitting it wide open. Must have happened fast and caught him by surprise. My guys will take the body away when you two are done."

"The killer's car left a lot of skid marks, but nothing good enough to make prints," said one of the forensic team.

"Hope you can catch him," said the ME. "Good luck."

They watched him go get in his car and drive away.

Smart turned to look at the body again. "Whoever did this deserves to die."

"I agree," said Stoddard. "Hate we got
to tell his wife what killed him, it's

grotesque, and we don't have much to go on."

***

By mere chance, Dietrich, instead of heading back to the city of DC when leaving the Lynn's house, went in the opposite direction, and meandered around aimlessly until he found his way across the beltway to Tysons Corners. It was bustling with people, but the parking lots were not near capacity, so he pulled into an open spot not too far from an entrance. He needed to calm down and do some thinking. He was hungry, too. He had not eaten anything all day, and it was very close to noon. There would be a restaurant in the mall somewhere. He was glad he'd stopped to get out of his blood spattered clothes in some bushes beside the road before coming. He even had brought a second pair of shoes in his suitcase. He had stashed the ruined garments a good way back into the woods, but he'd put the bloody ax in the trunk of the car. There was also some blood in the car, but that would have to wait. Right now, he decided to go find a place to eat. He parked, got out of his car and walked into the mall.

***

"I keep missing the guy," Dan complained as he drove Katheen home from the Lynn's. "I know he had been at Mia's house before I got there, and then I didn't get back here in time to catch him either. I'm glad you were here and watched, sweetheart."

"Lotta good it did for me to watch, but I wasn't about to let him see me when I saw that ax."

"We have to find him before he kills someone with it, if he hasn't already."

"The man was in a raging mad frenzy; out of his mind, Dan, very scary."

The short drive next door didn't take long, and Dan parked the Mustang in his garage. "When Dietrich left, where do you think he went?"

"Good question," said Kathleen as she took his hand, and walked into the house. "But I did notice he headed toward the beltway."

"A much faster way around DC," Dan replied. "It's time for lunch. We can talk about what to do next while we eat. I'm hungry."

Kathleen smiled, "I'm always hungry."

Dan rolled his eyes, "Don't I know, but I'm glad you're over that morning sickness." Kathleen was only two months into her pregnancy, so she wasn't showing yet.

Lunch was in full swing as they entered. The big dining table in the formal dining room was set, but not with formal ware. The whole household staff would be

eating with them. The food was just being served, so Dan and Kathleen joined
them. Dan sat at the head as usual, but Kathleen sat immediately to his right.

Eventually, the conversation lulled, and Dan said, "Clara, I wonder if you can think of what Dietrich might do next? You, too, Mia. I want to find him as soon as I can."

Clara put down her fork, and demurred. "I am so ashamed that I ever allowed him into my life even the first time. He was so big and handsome and charming; I was flattered he was attracted to me. He truly has become a monster. Though he was verbally abusive before, he was not so bad until he became the conductor of the Frankfurt Symphony Orchestra. That is when his enormous ego surfaced. He became an arrogant tyrant and he became physically abusive. We did separate a few times over the years, but he drew me back with false promises." She looked at Mandy, and said, "I'm sorry, but I was with him when he kidnapped you, Mandy, and I participated. I truly regret not trying to stop him, but he had already taken you before I found out." She turned again to Dan. "I hardly noticed the change in him just before the abduction. Then it seemed too late. Mom and I became estranged after Dietrich and I married and moved to Germany. He hadn't known about our child before, but when he learned he had a daughter that became a world class pianist, that's when he really began to get out of control. I'm afraid I have no idea where he might have gone or what he is doing, or might do."

"Well, neither do I, Dan," said Mia.

Kathleen cleared her throat and leaned forward. "Clara, I know Dietrich came to DC when you were 15, and I know he was here when he found you again and married you, and I know he has come to be a guest conductor of the Symphony Orchestra; I know all that, but I don't know how long he was here on those occasions when he was here in America, and I don't know how familiar he's become with DC over the years. Does he know his way around the city very well?"

"What a great question, sweetheart," said Dan.

Clara answered, "Why, yes, he does, now you've mentioned it."

Kathleen continued, "Are there any places he particularly likes to send some time?"

Clara pondered. "Malls," she said.

"He loves to spend time at malls."

"Since he was in this area," Kathleen continued, "do you think he might have gone over to Tysons Mall?"

"Yes," said Clara. "It is certainly a possibility. It is lunch time, and I am sure he would like to find food."

"The mall is very big," offered Dan. "He might be very hard to find among so may people."

"No," said Clara. "He loves food courts. If he is at a mall, you may be sure he is at a food court."

"Then, let's get over there now," said Dan as he stood.

Quickly, Dan, Kathleen, Mia and Clara loaded themselves, and drove away.

CHAPTER 30

The food court seemed the fastest and easiest place to grab a bite to eat, and besides that, he could sit where he could enjoy seeing all the people milling about. He was an avid people watcher, and he loved mall food courts. He had finished eating, and was relaxing with a fresh cup of coffee, and idly looked at passersby.

His passive mind began to wander back in time. He recalled the first time he ever saw Clara. She was so beautiful, and he had no idea she was so young. She looked to be full grown, not just fifteen. At that time, he was tall, dark, and handsome, as the cliche says. He was also slim. He did indeed seduce her, but returned to Germany very soon after to pursue his chosen career in music. Then, after becoming the conductor of the Frankfurt Symphony Orchestra, he came to America again as a guest conductor for the National Symphony Orchestra in Washington, DC. He stumbled upon Clara again. She and her mother, Mia, had attended the performance, and managed to accidently meet up. Clara was grown and beautiful. In time, they became lovers, and married. When she finally told him after he took her to Germany, that he had a daughter, that's what started this whole mess. Life had been so good before. Now he had to have Mandy. As father and daughter, they would take the classical music world by storm.

He suddenly remembered killing that policeman. He'd hacked him to death with Mia's ax. He'd been in a blind rage, and hardly recalled the incident. What had he done? He had killed an innocent man. He had never intended to do anyone harm, except Mia and Clara. Now he'd killed someone at random. A stranger. What should he do now?

Should he go into hiding? Where could he go?

Rationality began to cause him to relax, and try to think things through. It suddenly dawned on him that he had missed several rehearsals, and had deserted his post as conductor to fly to America and kidnap, Mandy. Nor had he made arrangements to take time off to go to America this time. He wondered if he still had a job. That is what he must do first, try to keep his job as conductor of a world class symphony orchestra. Otherwise kidnapping Mandy had no purpose. He suddenly stood up to look for a pay phone. No, he needed to go back to Miia's house to
make an overseas call. He would just barge in on her maids so he could use her phone. He didn't care if they tried to stop him. He was not to be stopped.

As Dietrich walked back out to his car, he wrestled with the thought of how he might explain his erratic behavior to the principals of the symphony, and explain where he was now, and why he was in America. Then he began to fear he may have already been fired. He didn't notice the big station wagon enter the lot, nor did Dan and his passengers notice the nondescript rental car drive out of the parking lot. He took the beltway back around DC to I-95, and drove as fast as he could within the speed limit.

He was nearing his exit for Woodbridge when he saw the little red sportscar in his rear view mirror. It must be coming at about a 100 miles an hour when it swerved to pass him and barely clipped his rear fender. At 75 miles an hour, his car went into a wild spin. He heard screaming, but it came from his own throat. He tried to turn his wheels into the spin, but that only caused him to lose control entirely. He felt as though he was falling. The sudden impact into the concrete barrier released the airbag into his face. There was a sound of the bag's release, and of ripping metal as the

car swung completely around to face the wrong
direction. The driver's door came wide
open, and he rolled out of the car onto the verge.

Instinct kicked in, and he quickly got up, rushed to the back of the car. The trunk was already open from the impact. He grabbed the bloody ax and his suitcases, and hurried away from the wreckage into the woods along the road that led to Mia's house.

When he felt he was safely hidden from view, he stopped to take inventory of himself. He was shaking violently, and his legs felt weak and wobbly. His clothes were dirty, of course, but he could find no blood or injuries on himself. He had been incredibly lucky to have survived at all. He sat down on a large branch that was on the ground. He was close enough to the highway to hear the sirens, and the shouting around the accident, but he was hidden from view.

Unknown to the first responders to the accident, the little red sportscar was long gone with only slight damage to its right front fender.

No one was in or near the wrecked rental car. The car's rental agency told the police that a Mr. Dietrich Schmidt had rented the car, so the police sent an all-points bulletin out to locate him. Eventually the small amounts of blood were noticed in the trunk, but it would be quite a while before a match would be found. Also, a search for Dietrich Schmidt had to be organized.

While all that was going on, Dietrich made his way through the thick underbrush for some distance, then stopped. He spent some time trying to clean himself up. Then he went straight to Mia's house, and was able to sneak into her garage and hang the ax back in its place. None of her maids saw or heard him, so he quickly walked away. He looked at the time on his watch. It was after three in the afternoon. He calculated that it would be about time in the morning in Frankfurt when the symphony personnel would be just starting their day. He had to go back to save his job, or all he'd done was wasted..

He found a pay phone at a strip mall and phoned for a taxi. When the taxi arrived, he went to Dulles and bought a ticket to Frankfurt under his real name, the name he'd used when he came; Sondheim. For the rental car, he'd used his fake identity as Schmidt.

He sat to wait for his flight to be called. He would deal with other things after he was secure in his job.

CHAPTER 30

The car had crashed. It was destroyed, and the driver could not be found though the police had put out an "all points" bulletin for him and the rental car. Of course the name the rental car gave was not his real name. The rental agency was furious to have a wrecked car on their hands, and no one to hold accountable. They really wanted to get the man; Mr. Dietrich Schmidt, but he seemed to have vanished into thin air.

Again, as coincidences go, Woodbridge was the community nearest the accident, so Dianna Smart and James Stoddard were assigned to this situation as well as the patrolman that was hacked to death with an ax. They had no idea the two cases were in any way connected.

Smart was driving, and as they turned into the parking lot at Dulles International, a gentle rain began to fall.

"Don't worry," she said, "I have an umbrella on the floor of the back seat."

"I'll get it," said Stoddard as he turned and reached a long arm down to pick it up. He was rakishly tall, and seemed to be all elbows and knees. He had a mop of brownish curly hair, and was dressed in a gray suit, black tie, and white shirt.

"After you park, I'll come around to
your side to get you under it. Wouldn't
want to let that beautiful hairdo to get wet."

Smart ignored him. She was five foot two, a slender young woman, thirty five years old, with shoulder-length mousey-brown hair, tied in a ponytail. She was quite attractive. It wasn't a long walk into the terminal, and Stoddard, a twenty eight year old, was folding up the umbrella just as they approached the car rental counter.

To greet them was a young man of twenty-something standing behind the counter.

Smart took the lead, of course, "Are you the one who waited on Mr. Schmidt who's rental car was destroyed?"

"Mr. Schmidt? No ma'am," he replied. "let me get my supervisor. Maybe she can help you." He walked away.

A member of management accompanied the young clerk upon his return, and wanted to rant a bit about their damaged car, so it took a bit of time to get the actual clerk who had waited on Schmidt to come talk to them.

She was a bright young lady, mid-twenties, blond colored hair to her shoulders. She wore a simple little green
Dress uniform of the agency. She had a

lovely warm smile.

"Hi," she said, "I'm Wanda Graham. I waited on Mr. Schmidt. He'd just landed, I assume from Germany, because he had a very thick German accent."

Smart jumped on it, "Wait, you said he'd just landed?"

"Yes, ma'am, that's what he said."

Stoddard whipped out a small note pad and pen. "Could you possibly describe him?"

She grinned, "Easy. He was a very big man. At least six foot four; maybe taller. I'd guess he must have weighed nearly four hundred pounds."

"Wow," said Stoddard as he wrote furiously on his pad. Wanda really looked Stoddard over, and barely stifled a little giggle.

Smart asked, "How was he dressed?"

She turned her eyes toward Smart. "He wore a casual shirt with flowers all over

it. Must have been made by Omar
the
tentmaker." She giggled again. "His
pants
were black, and his shirt was not
tucked in.
I don't remember seeing his shoes.
　　"Oh, and he was carrying two
large
suitcases," she added.
　　"Do you have any idea which
airline he'd come in on?"
　　"No ma'am."
Smart turned to Stoddard, and said,
"Let's go see if we can find out which
airline he
used."
　　After almost two hours, they
could not find any German flight that
had a Dietrich Schmidt on board.
　　"Don't see this getting us
anywhere,"
said Smart. "We've covered them all.
It's as
though he *didn't* just fly in."
　　"That is strange," said
Stoddard. He

must have lied about just flying in. Then he suddenly said, "Hey! What if we describe Schmidt to the ticket agents? Maybe he flew in under an assumed name, but his physical appearance is memorable, to say the least."

"That's a great idea, James. You see? Sometimes you *are* useful."

It didn't take them long to find the agent that remembered the big man, and there, they learned his real name, Schneider. They further learned he was a world famous symphony conductor, and he had also just flown back to Frankfurt. He had already landed there, but they believed he would be easily and quickly apprehended in Germany. Extradition could be arranged, they hoped.

***

Dietrich went straight to his home upon landing in Frankfurt, and when he called Lars Gerhardt, the general manager of the Symphony only to learn he'd indeed he'd lost his job. He had been replaced temporarily by his associate conductor, Ludmilla Neumann, while they searched for his permanent replacement. He flew into a great rage again. He roared like a wounded wildebeest, and threw the telephone across the room with such force, the cord was jerked out of the wall. The servants fled into the far corners of the big house. None wanted to be anywhere near him when he was in one of his states.

Suddenly, he stopped. He had a brilliant idea. He went out to his car, pulled out of the garage, and sped away toward a part of downtown Frankfurt where he'd gotten his alias and documents as Dietrich Schmidt.

CHAPTER 31

After lunch, Dan told all his guests, "I'll keep close tabs on all of you and your houses. I've called my Dallas office to send five detectives up to DC. Dietrich seems to be in the wind again. I think you can all go back to your homes. Someone will be watching your house and apartment."

"Well," said Tom, "now I can get repairs started."

"And I can go get ready for my concert next month, except my piano has been destroyed," said Mandy.

"Don't worry, sweetheart," said Tom to his daughter. Mom and I will take you to Whittles to pick out a new one. It was insured."

"I don't know of any other aliases Dietrich might have, but I am sure it is possible," said Clara.

"We will have to keep a watchful eye, too, Clara," said Mia.

"I'll stay with you, mom, but I want to find a place of my own soon."

Clara was her birth mother, so she said, "My apartment is still mine, but I'm moving back home for a while, you can rent it if you like, Clara," she suddenly realized she had not called her mother, but she continued, "It isn't large, but I found it adequate and comfortable. I'll have to return the grand piano so you'll have more room," she laughed.

Clara brightened, "Oh, Mandy, I'd love to see it. Could we go now?"

"Of course," said Mandy, "my car is just outside. I drove it over when we came over to stay at Dan's."

Mandy and Clara left, followed by Tom and Mary, then Mia reluctantly left, not really wanting to go home alone. Of course her household staff were still there.

After seeing them all off, Kathleen turned to Dan and said, "Alone at last."

Dan smiled.

***

On the drive, Mandy, kept glancing at Clara and thinking, *"I can't get used to her as my actual mother, but I need to try. She seems very sweet."*

Clara felt Mandy's eyes on her, and eventually commented, "I am sure you are having a hard time accepting me as your real mother, and I understand completely. Now I am very sorry I ever gave you up for adoption, but my mother insisted; I was
just fifteen. You were raised with Mary as
your mother. It will take time for you to get used to two mothers, but I want you to know how happy I am to finally meet you, and I am so very proud of you. I am so looking forward to your concert next month. However, I know I have a bit of a German accent since I've lived there since I was twenty three, but I do speak English." She turned and

smiled at Mandy.

Mandy glanced at her, and smiled back, "I know, and you are so right. We can work this out together. . . mom." Clara leaned over, and gave Mandy a hug. It felt good for both of them.

Then Clara began to think how angry her husband would be now, and she wondered where he was, and what he might do. He'd seemed to have disappeared. The very thought of him made her shudder.

***

Mia felt a little sad as she drove to her house in Woodbridge alone. She so longed for her daughter and granddaughter to be with her, but she was also happy she and Clara managed to help Mandy escape back to America.

The closer she came to her home, the more she hoped that monstrous pig would not be there waiting for her, and that her girls

were still ok. She wondered how long it might be until one of Dan's detectives
would be there watching her house, and protecting her from her son-in-law.

As she came in sight of her house, there was a strange car parked out front. She wondered who it might be. She hoped it wasn't Dietrich., yet she drove right into her garage. almost immediately she noticed her ax on the wall. It looked like there was a little blood on the ax head.

When she entered her house, she found two strangers sitting in her parlor having coffee. She was glad it wasn't Dietrich. They stood as she entered, and Emelia said, "Mrs. Becker, so glad you came home. These detectives want to talk to you about Mr. Dietrich."

"Hello, Mrs. Becker," said detective Smart. "I'm Dianna Smart, and this is James Stoddard. We would like to ask you a few questions about your son-in-law."

They shook hands and sat back down. Mia sat across from the detectives, and her maids left.

She laid her purse on the floor beside her chair, and asked, "What do you want to know?"

"First, do you have any idea where he is right now?"

"I'm afraid I don't. What is this about?"

"It seems Mr. Sondheim has murdered an officer of the law, and we are trying to find him," said Stoddard.

Mia was stunned, and both her hands clamped on her mouth.

"Murdered!" She then put a hand to her breast. "I... I.. d... didn't know," she stammered. Then she remembered. "He... he hacked up a house in McLean just a while ago with an ax. Did quite a bit of damage. A friend watched him do it, but we had no idea he'd killed anyone. He'd used an ax I had in my garage for chopping fire wood in the winters, and by the way, he's returned it. It is now hanging in my

Garage again, and it looks like there is blood on it."

"What?" exclaimed detective smart, and she and Stoddard suddenly stood.

"If that is the ax he used to kill that trouper, then we must confiscate it as evidence," said Smart, and they all three went into Mia's garage. There was the ax, and it was quite bloody along the blade, though it was now dried blood. Stoddard slipped on some plastic gloves, and took the ax down. He and Smart looked at it closely. Then Stoddard took the ax out to their car to put in in the trunk.

Smart looked at Mia, and said, "There must be much more to your story, Mrs. Becker. Let's go back inside, and you tell us everything."

When Stoddard returned, they all sat down, and Mia told them everything that had happened. When she told about Mandy's kidnapping, she told of the FBI working with Tom and Mary Lynn, and Dan Good's involvement. The detectives said they would arrange a meeting with the

FBI, and they also wanted to talk to
Dan Good.

CHAPTER 32

Thursday, September 18, 1986

Max Becker felt it was shear genius that he'd gotten this new alias, and had booked a flight back to Washington, DC. Becker was his mother-in law's name, and that's just who he wanted to visit very soon after he landed. He liked his new alias.

Dietrich smiled at his cleverness. He had lost his dream job as a world class symphony conductor, and all hope of performing with his prodigy daughter. His life was in shambles, and it was all Mia's fault. His fury was almost more than he could bar. He wished he still had that ax. He would chop her to pieces. Perhaps he could get it, or maybe just buy another. Now, however, he could only sit back in his widow seat, and watch the clouds below, and wait.

As he waited, Dietrich began thinking of making new plans. Now he had no job; perhaps he should move to the US and find a new career of some kind, but what? He had lived his dream, having always wanting to be a conductor of a renown symphony orchestra. Now it seemed it was just a dream as he remembered his journey in music. Music had always been his life. He knew he could not live without it; but he also knew he must now live in the shadows. He'd killed a man, so whatever he chose to do in life, he must never again enjoy notoriety. He must be invisible if he settled in America. Then he thought, perhaps he should find a different nation; Switzerland, or one of the South American countries. As a child, his chosen instrument had been piano, just as Mandy, his daughter, had chosen. He *could* just teach private piano lessons. He actually hated children, but it was still something he could do and remain almost completely anonymous. He would just have to learn to deal with children. He suddenly felt it had to be in America, he still had to take care of Mia, and Clara, and perhaps others.

Yes! He would settle in America. He would sell his house in Frankfurt. That would give him plenty of money to get started. But where could he live until he could make all the proper arrangements? He smiled. He just had an idea.

Then, another thought came to him.

How can I disguise myself so nobody can recognize me?

When the big plane landed at Dulles International, Dietrich, now known as Max Becker quickly grabbed his bags, and found a taxi to take him to the hotel on Dupont Circle in DC. Along the way, he had the taxi stop at a drugstore where he purchased some blond hair die, and some makeup. Then he had the taxi take him to the hotel.

The sky was quite gray, and there was a bit of a nip in the air, and the smell of autumn spoke of the change in the weather that was approaching.

Once in his suite, he died his hair and deftly touched up a few pock marks on his face. He looked at himself over in the mirror. He looked at least ten years younger, maybe twenty, he thought. He was certainly a different person; except for his size. He had to lose weight. Then he returned to unpack his two suitcases. He selected casual slacks, and shirt. What he'd done so far would suffice as a disguise. He was exhausted from the long time in the air, and changing his appearance, so he laid on one of the twin beds to rest. Soon, he was asleep.

***

A sudden horn toot made them all freeze. They looked at each other, and then went to look out a front window. It was Dan and Kathleen parking out front. They got out, and walked casually up to Mia's front door.

"Hi, Mia," said Kathleen.

Mia greeted them, then said, "I have something to tell you." She turned to her cook, "Anna, make us a fresh pot of coffee, please, and see if there are some cookies."

"Great," said Dan, and soon they were
all seated in the parlor with coffee and a plate stacked high with large chocolate chip cookies.

Mia sat back and said, "Now let me tell you *my* news. When you two drove up, two detectives had just driven away. They wanted to know if I knew where my son-in-law, Dietrich, was. I told them I didn't know. Then they told me he'd murdered a Highway Patrolman hacked him to death with an ax; my ax, actually."

"Oh My!" said Kathleen. "Hacked to death with an ax? How awful."

"I know. I couldn't believe he had killed a man. I knew he could be violent, but to kill someone? Couldn't believe he'd murdered someone.; and a Highway Patrol Officer. He had used my ax! I saw it when I drove into the garage, and noticed it looked like it had dried blood on it. I told the detectives about it, and they took it as evidence to analyze the blood. Then I told them of Mandy's kidnapping back on September first. I told them the FBI was called in, then I told them of your involvement, and that Mandy had been freed, and was now safely at home with her parents. They said they would contact the FBI, and that they wanted to talk to you, too, Dan."

"I guess it was inevitable, especially after a murder," said Dan. "I'll be ready to talk to them."

"The detectives didn't seem to know who Dietrich Sondheim was, and I didn't tell them. To them it was just a name," said Mia.

Kathleen smiled, "Peasants."

CHAPTER 33

It was late afternoon, and Dietrich had parked off into the bushes down the street from Mia's house so his rental car was at least not so conspicuous. He sneaked through the underbrush just close enough to see a very tall man and a beautiful woman get out of a big car, and walk up to Mia as she stood on her front porch. She welcomed them with a big smile, and they went inside. He cursed under his breath. Who were these people? He'd never seen them before.

In greater anger now, he went back to his rental car and drove away. As he was passing a strip mall, he saw a small hardware store, and parked. Inside, he purchased a nice sharp ax. From the time he'd first envisioned hacking Mia and

Clara into little pieces with the one he'd taken from Mia's garage; he thought an ax was, for him, the weapon that would be the most satisfying method of killing them both.

Besides, it was easier to purchase than a gun, and would do much more damage than just a knife. The clerk had wrapped it well, and since it was not obvious what he'd purchased, he took it to his car, and put it in the trunk. As he drove back to his hotel on Dupont Circle, there was only one thing on his mind; murder.

***

Dick Leigh had just recently made friends with a new kid in high school this first semester of the year, Bill Buck, and Bill had taken a shine to Dick. They were both Boy Scouts, and enjoyed hiking, so on this Saturday morning in mid-September, Bill asked Dick to go hiking with him. He knew a spot in the Woodbridge woods where there was a creek that had a good sized pool where they could go skinny dipping. Bill had dark brown hair, and was an army brat who had lived all over the world, but Dick, a blond, had never been anywhere. Bill was a big boy. At 17 he was six foot one, and weighed 195. Dick was 16, five foot seven, and very thin, weighing only 118.

Bill drove up to Dick's house, picked him up, and drove in the direction of I-95, but stopped about half a mile away, pulling off the road a short way into the woods. They got their backpacks and Bill led the way.

In a quarter of an hour, they came to the creek, and followed it till they found where the creek had backed up to form a nice pond they could swim in. They dropped their backpack, and began stripping off their clothes.

Bill laughed when he saw just how skinny Dick was. "You would have to stand twice just to make a shadow."

"Yeah? And you look like a tub o'
lard," quipped Dick.

"Last one in is a sissy," yelled
Bill as he turned and ran to dive in
the water. Dick was not far behind,
and yelled back, "No fair, I never had
a chance."

The boys frolicked and splashed
each other, swimming and diving.
After about an hour they climbed out
and lay on the grass a while to get
dry. After they dressed, they began
hiking back to Bill's car, but they
took a bit of a circuitous route, and
Dick suddenly stopped. "Hey, Bill."

He stopped and turned around.
"What?"

"Look," said Dick. "Somebody
left a big pile of clothes over yonder."
He pointed to his right.

"Yeah, let's check it out."

Bill picked up a man's suit coat
first. "Look at the size of this thing.
The guy is taller than I am."

"Yeah," said Dick, "but what's
all that stuff on it?"

"Looks like dried blood to me," said Dick.

"Blood! Yuk!" Bill dropped the jacket.

Dick began picking up and examining the rest of the clothes. Every item had spattered blood, and he held up the trousers, "This guy's a giant."

"Nah," said Bill, "but we better call the cops. They need to see this."

The two boys went directly to Dick's house, and called the Woodbridge police.

The bloody clothes of Dietrich Sondheim would only strengthen the case of murder against him.

***

Clara had been delighted that she was able to take over Mandy's lease of the apartment. It was perfect for her, she thought. It was so nice of Mandy to suggest such an arrangement that worked out so well for each of them.

She was finally getting the little added touches to the place to make it seem more like home to her; her nick-nacks and pictures, especially photographs of her childhood, her mother and father. Then she found a photo of her wedding. She stopped and sat heavily on her couch. Marrying Dietrich had been a terrible mistake. She believed that at the age of thirty-nine she was still an attractive woman, and could still find a good husband, but she would be more careful this time. Now, she reflected, that she'd found her daughter, life would be really good. Suddenly, she shuddered. Dietrich was still free, and that terrified her. A though came to her unbidden, then she made an impetuous decision. She wanted nothing more to do with him. Her mother had money, and would help her divorce his very soon. The opened the frame, took out the photo and ripped it up, and threw it all in the trash. Enough was enough, and she was going to divorce him, especially now since he had become a murderer.

CHAPTER 34

Friday, September 19, 1986

Clouds were rolling in from the Northwest, and the sky was darkening to a pall of gray, blotting out the morning sunrise over Washington, DC. The patter of rain hit the windshield as he drove, and in a short time, he began to hear a rolling thunder, and a hard rain descended in sheets, blown by a strong wind. He turned the wipers on full, but could barely see through the downpour. He hadn't dressed for a rainy day. He wore a Hawaiian shirt that was not too flashy in a green floral pattern. His slacks were a light tan, and his loafers had been polished to a glossy shine. He had no umbrella. This was not good. He had no idea the weather could change so fast. He should have dressed warmer and worn a coat.

Suddenly he heard a siren screaming in the distance. He quickly checked his speed. He was driving well within the speed limit. It couldn't be a police car. He guessed it must be a fire engine or ambulance. The sound was getting louder, so he began watching for flashing lights. Perhaps he should just turn around and go back to his hotel and try later. He hated getting soaked. No, he would continue on. He would decide what to do   when he got there. Perhaps the rain will let up soon. The fire truck came into view. He slowed and pulled over to let it pass. Other emergency vehicles also sped by. Then he resumed speed.

It was half past ten when he rolled to a stop about fifty yards from Mia's big house. It was still raining, but wasn't as bad as it had been. The dark clouds and rain shrouded the house in gloom. He picked up the binoculars from the passenger seat to get a closer look. A few lights were on throughout the house.

Then Mia walked out on the front porch. The large covered porch extended across the width of the house. She wore a heavy jacket against the cold wind. and she stood watching the rain for a moment. Then she turned to look down the street and saw a car parked on the side of the street, but it was pretty far down and she could not see if it was occupied because of the rain.

She saw a car parked quite away down from her house. It made her shiver. Then she went back inside.

***

That strange car could be Dietrich, She wasn't about to be caught unaware and unprepared if it was him. "Girls! Be sure all the windows and doors are locked," shouted Mia as she came inside. She walked quickly up the stairs to the second floor and into her bedroom. In a dresser drawer she found her binoculars that were high quality and powerful. Then she went to an upstairs window that looked down on the part of the street in front of her house where she could look at that car. As luck would have it, the rain had diminished to a drizzle, so she saw a blond-headed man at the wheel. It wasn't Dietrich, he wasn't blond. Nothing to worry about, she thought. She could just relax and go take a nap. Still, she wondered who it could be and why was he sitting in a car where he was. There was nothing there but woods; no houses anywhere near. It troubled her, but she went back to her bedroom. Instead of lying down, she made a phone call.

***

He was happy the rain had slowed to a drizzle, and hoped it would soon stop. Dietrich opened the trunk and slipped out of the car to walk to the back, got the ax.

He crossed over to the other side of the street, the side Mia's house was on, and disappeared into the woods. He would sneak up on her from the back of her house. The air was quite cool, but the wind was not bad.

The thickness of the underbrush through the woods was making his approach very difficult. The going was slow. The darkness wasn't quite so dark anymore, still it was hard to see his way. The trees dripped heavily, and water ran down his face into his eyes. In fact, he felt he was getting disoriented. He suddenly realized he had no sense of direction. He was lost.

He stopped and looked up at the sky. The rain had finally stopped completely, but the clouds were still very dark. Too dark to be trapsing through the underbrush. He felt himself a fool to have decided on this approach to Mia's house. Perhaps he should turn back. But which way? He'd lost all sense of direction. In his frustration, he began to curse out loud in German, but his shouts were muffled in the dense, wet, foliage.

As he fumed, the sky began growing lighter. The wind was picking up again, and colder. The clouds were moving rapidly and getting thinner. The weather definitely was changing.. It wasn't too long until Dietrich could see through the trees and spotted Mia's big house. He was surprised he wasn't very far away. He began to head that direction with his ax, but the wet woods and muddy ground was
a frustrating hindrance. His nice new loafers were caked with thick mud. His
shoes were ruined. The big man was also somewhat surprised at just how dense the Virginia foliage was, but it wasn't long till he broke through to her back yard, From this point, the house was about thirty yards away.

***

Mia was still standing at the corner

window looking down the street. That strange car was still there, but the blond headed man was gone. She wondered where he went. Then she noticed Clara's car coming her way. She was very pleased her daughter was coming to see her, but wondered why. She wasn't
expecting her. She wished she'd called before coming. Oh well, she thought she would be happy to see her. Forgetting about the blond stranger, she put her binoculars away, and went downstairs to meet her daughter. It was wonderful that she now lived in America, and she could see her anytime and often.

"Hi, sweetheart," called Mia from the front porch as Clara stepped out of her car in the circular driveway.

"Hi, mom, I decided to come for a visit; hope you don't mind my showing up unexpectedly."

"Of course not. I couldn't be more
pleased. It's wonderful you live so near

now. Not way off in Germany
anymore. Come on in, can you stay
for lunch?"

Clara didn't answer until they
had both entered the foyer. "Sure,
mother. I came to tell you I found a
job, and start work tomorrow, so I
won't have many opportunities like
today."

"Oh? What kind of job did you
get?"

"I'm so excited! I'm going to be a
translator at the State Department; I
start Monday."

Their conversation continued for
a few minutes, then Clara's face
darkened as she said, "I have not
heard a word from Dietrich in some
time, have you?"

"No," said Mia, "and I have been
concerned. I wonder where he is and
what
he is up to."

"It isn't like him to forget about
us, he
was in such a rage; and he's killed a
man."

"I know, and the police are looking for him."

"I'm scared, mother."

"There has been a strange car just sitting down the street; did you notice it as you drove by it?"

"I didn't, why?"

"I've been uneasy since I first saw it this morning. I was afraid it was Dietrich, but it was a blond-headed man. Then he disappeared from the car. I have no idea where he might have gone, but he has been gone a long time."

Clara shuddered. "That scares me, mother."

Chapter 35

As you entered the front double doors to Mia's house, the foyer was large. The floors were white marble, and gorgeous chandelier hung from the center of the entryway ceiling. Just inside, and to the left was an umbrella stand and a large antique coat tree. To the right was an arched opening in to a formal livingroom. The furniture was sumptuous, and was dotted with more antiques. Many beautiful and large original oil paints with gilded frames were abundant throughout, and there were numerous large plants an small Ficus trees as well. Virtually everything was white. To the left was another archway to a large dining room. Straight ahead was a broader archway into a great room, longer than wide, so there was a door to the left into a smaller dining room for six. On the right was the parlor. In the great room was a table just inside on the right to accommodate mail, a landline telephone with a chair, and other small items. Next to the table, a big rolltop desk sat with a comfortable-looking executive, white leather roll-chair. There were other assorted tables and chairs scattered around; some antiques. At the back of the great room was another smaller archway into a square hallway with walls. In the right wall a double door opened int the kitchen. It was quite large with the finest appliances, and a good sized breakfast nook in one corner. The door on the left led into a small, but comfortable suite for the cook and her husband, if she had one, which Mia's cook did not. The suite had an attached bathroom, and a small sitting room Straight ahead from the great room was a door to the laundry room; then the mud room and the back door. In the great room were the stairs to the second floor. Upstairs were five nice suites with a bathroom and a small sitting room. There was a large den where the stairs entered, but the house had no basement.

Mia and Clara sat in the breakfast nook. Mia had a cup if tea, and Clara had a diet soda. They were discussing lunch with Ada, the cook. Her other maids and housekeepers were nowhere to be seen.

***

His clothes were soaked, his hair plastered to his head, and he was shivering cold. It only made him more furious. He could hardly wait to get his hands on Mia and Clara; he'd seen her drive up. It would all
be done soon. The longer he looked at the house, the more angry he became.

He shook his head to expel some water, and shook his arms to expel some anxiety. All reason was gone as he charged the house, screaming with rage. At the door, he made no

effort to see if it was locked or unlocked. Immediately he swung the ax with abandon, not caring where he hit. The glass shattered, splintering the
wood and making a gap. Then he swung it again and again until the door was gaping open enough he could enter.

***

should Dietrich try to break into her house. "Hide," was her code word for everyone in her house to go to their designated places. Just one more day, and Dan's detective from Dallas would arrive to protect them, but Dietrich had surprised them.

***

The crashing sound of glass breaking, and wood splintering made Mia, Clara, and Ada nearly jump out of their skin. Of course they were all a little wary about the blond-headed man that had disappeared, so they were unaware Dietrich was anywhere near. The women had no doubt it was Dietrich frantically smashing in the back door, so Mia shouted, "Hide!" Mia had devised a plan He heard an off-key chorus of screams as he lumbered into the mud room, through the laundry room and into the kitchen. His eyes darted around frantically. It was empty. He searched everywhere. Where had they gone? It was such a big house they could be anywhere. He wasn't interested in Mia's staff, but he would not hesitate to kill them all if necessary, but it was Mia and Clara he wanted. He couldn't hear a sound in the house. He was sure they were all hiding somewhere. He'd been here many times, and knew the house well, he would have to hunt them down.

There were many places to hide on the first floor, and he was cautious as he searched. He began to wonder if they had devised some method of defense against him. He was entering the great room, but it

was very open; few places to hide except behind couches and large chairs, bit as he moved toward the front of the house, there were two large closets. He silently sneaked up to one door, raised the ax high to strike, threw yje door open, but there was no one. He approached the second coset door the same way, and with the same result. Neither were the hiding in the two dining rooms to his right, ore the main livingroom. The hall closet was also empty of women, so
he went up the stairs as quietly as he could.

Dietrich searched for the women upstairs as slowly and cautiously as he had
the downstairs with the same result. No one seemed to be in the house at all, but he'd heard them scream and run. Had he missed them? Were there other hiding places he knew nothing about? He decided to go back and search through the entire dwelling again.

They could not possibly be anywhere in the house, but where could they have gone?

Outside, of course, you dolt!

This realization revived his rage to an even higher level if that was possible. He rushed to the front doors, but the double doors were locked. The fools had locked him in! He tore into the doors at their latches with his ax, and crashed out on the front porch to look around. Clara's car was still there, and he raced around the house to see Mia's car was where it was, so they had not driven off. He knew he'd not heard any cars outside.

Quickly he searched the grounds around her house, then realized they must have sneaked into the woods across the street.

***

The density of the Virginia countryside is daunting it is so thick. Even all the way up to the roadways it looks absolutely impossible to enter. Many would not think they could get into it at all without a machete to hack their way in, and such was the case of the woods across the street from Mia's house.

After Mia had locked the front doors, the women scampered across the street and somehow made their way into the thick woods. They were all wearing jackets. They moved far into the brush to be sure he could not see them from the house. When they came to a small clearing, they stopped.

"This gives us the advantage," said Mia. "We are higher up, and we can look down all around us. We will see him coming from any direction."

"What happened? Did Dietrich sneak up on us? I thought you only saw some strange car down the street with a blond-headed man in it," asked Clara.

"I don't know," answered Mia. "When we all ran across the street, I didn't see any other car. I don't know where he came from."

"It's no doubt it is him," concluded Clara. "I'd know that voice anywhere."

Mia's domestic girls coward together
in terror. They all thought they were about to die.

Suddenly, one of the girls said, "What's that noise?"

Mia turned to put a gentle hand on
her arm, "It's just Dietrich, Ada. He's figured out we're not hiding in the house, and realizes we must be somewhere outside. I locked the front doors, but instead of just opening it from the inside, he's chosen to hack down the door with that stupid ax. He'll be coming over here soon."

"What can we do?" asked Clara.

Mia smiled at her daughter, "Never mind, dear. I made a phone call just before
you came."

Chapter 36

Dietrich charged across the street into the underbrush swinging his ax like it was a machete, but it wasn't a machete, it was an ax; clumsy and awkward. It actually slowed his progress, which was fine with Mia's group. They watched him carefully. With savage fury, he fought his way into the dense thicket.

The sky was growing darker again, and a fog was rolling in, but Dietrich was too into his search for the women to notice.

Mia thought he looked ridiculous as he chopped his way through the foliage in his loud, wet Hawaiian shirt plastered to his body. That stupid blond hair was also plastered to his head. He looked silly.

She had called Dan Good because of the blond stranger that had parked down the street from her and then disappeared. Now she knew Dietrich had dyed his hair. It was just a precaution to call Dan when she did, but he agreed to come to her place. She hoped he would get here soon, but how would he know where they were? She'd not told him of her plan to hide in the woods across from her house. She'd been so pleased with herself that she'd called Dan, but now she was worried if he could find them before Dietrich did.

Suddenly she turned to the others and gestured for them to come close to her. When they were close, she whispered, "Everyone go as far away as you can, and hide. I'm going back to the house. I have to be there when Dan Good comes. I called him, and I must tell him where Dietrich is; now go."

Each woman turned and hurried deeper into the woods, and Mia turned toward her house, but wanted to circle around Dietrich.

From her position on the slight rise of the ground in the clearing, she could catch glimpses of him as he approached. It was slow going through the underbrush, but she pushed herself along as fast as she could.

She could not see that Dan had just driven up to her house. He stopped in front, and started to walk up to the front door when he saw the doors were splintered and sagging open. Quickly he reasoned that Dietrich must have come for them, and crashed the doors open, not to get in, but out of the house. He turned and ran toward the woods across the street. He could see the brush had been hacked away in a kind of trail. Immediately, he knew the women were in great danger.. a fog had rolled in,
and was growing thicker. He had to find them if it wasn't already too late. The good thing was that Dietrich had blazed a nice trail for him to follow, and his trek would be easier and faster.

Dietrich was frustrated in his search. He had no idea which was he was going, nor in which way he should go, so he stopped. He decided to look around for any evidence of the path the women had taken. As he turned to his right, his eye caught a glimpse of color and movement through the trees. Someone was trying to circle around behind him. It was serendipitous in the fog that he had seen the tan color moving some distance away, so he quickly began to move in that direction. Mia had worn her light tan jacket to wear into the woods. Dietrich was making good progress with his ax. He had become more proficient with experience, but Mia was slower, not realizing Dietrich was gaining on her. She looked up to see a foggy image of her house through the trees. She was almost there, but she did not see Dan's car parked in front of her house. She plunged on with more enthusiasm.

When the trail veered off to the right, Dan saw Dietrich about thirty yards ahead. He was wielding an ax to cut his way through the thicket. He was wearing a bright Hawaiian shirt, and his hair was now blond.

A noise behind her caused Mia to turn and look. It was Dietrich, and he was getting close. She turned to see she was almost free of the woods, and she let out a yelp. She wasn't going to make it. He would catch her and kill her.

Dan hear the high pitched cry of a female voice, and not knowing which woman it was, he knew she must have seen Dietrich drawing closer to her. He picked up his speed.

Dietrich caught up with Mia, and screamed at her, "I got you now!" She turned toward him as he raised his ax high over his head, but before he could move it, it came suddenly out of his hands, and a huge fist slammed into his temple like sledgehammer, knocking him unconscious. He lay on the ground, and Dan saw Mia's terrified face.

"It's over, Mia. You're safe now," he said with a warm smile on his face. "Call your ladies out."

"Come out now," she screamed. "Dietrich is down for the count."

Dan thought, *Man. She has a voice like a burglar.*

***

They had all gathered in the kitchen, Mia, Clara, and all Mia's staff. Dietrich had been taken away to jail, and Kathleen had driven over in her car to join in the celebrations. She had brought Mandy and Tom and Mary as well.

It was definitely turning into a dreary September day, but inside Mia's home, the atmosphere was bright and cheery.

"Dietrich will be charged with murder of the highway patrol officer, and attempted murder of you, Mia, and of course, Mandy's kidnapping just for starters. I have a great criminal lawyer," said Dan, and the celebrations began.

Printed in Great Britain
by Amazon